BLACK BUTTERFLY 2:

EBONI

MACHIAVELLI
"THE SEVEN DAY THEORY"

by
FEENIX

BLACK BUTTERFLY 2 by FEENIX

Black Butterfly II:

My name is Eboni, much like the life I lead... **Black**.

Hiding in the **back**... the _shadows_,

Nobody cares because nobody _knows_... **it's me**.

 Damn, why wouldn't life just **let me be?**

  Left alone, all I wanted was my son and a happy _home._

Maybe a car with a little _chrome_...

 A cedar chest, death by old age, weed & poetry to

cover pain of being _left alone_.

 So tell me...

Who should pay the **price** for a stolen **life?**

Broken dreams, _my child's needs_- sometimes I feel

like I _internally bleed_...from the edge of a jagged **knife**.

Now I know **the true definition of strife!**

BLACK BUTTERFLY 2 by FEENIX

INTRODUCTION:

"The Seven Day Theory"

7 months after the funeral of Baltimore's favorite actress and hood sweetheart, Eboni Burton...

"Nurse, Nurse! Damn, did somebody put me on a pay no mind list or something? I need a Nurse!" John sat up in the hospital bed and continued to press the buzzer for the nurse's station over and over again.

"Yes, Mr. James... you only have to press the buzzer one time, we can hear it. How may I help you?" The nurse was visibly agitated.

"You can help by sending me back home! I'm feeling a lot better. This place is a fuckin' prison!"

"As I told you earlier, Mr. James," the nurse was trying to remain patient with him, "We still have to run a few more tests to run. I'm going to need a little more blood from you, okay?"

"Fu-u-ck you! You've already bled me dry…"

"Yes, I know we've already taken samples, but for some reason they have been misplaced. Maybe they were lost in the shift change or something."

"Lost in the shift change? How does a hospital lose someone's blood? What kind of operation are you running around here? Nobody's sticking me again without my lawyer hearing about this shit." John rolled his eyes and rudely turned over onto his stomach without saying another word.

"Okay Mr. James, have it your way," responded the nurse as she threw her hands in the air and left the room.

"Good! Hey, turn the goddamn light off while you're at it," shouted John.

The nurse stuck her hand back in, turned off the light, and hurried to her desk as she grinded her teeth together. Soon as she arrived at the nurse's station, she was sure to tell the other nurses to ignore him the rest of the night and even turned down the volume on the call box.

"Nurse Mary!" The doctor on duty startled her with his abrasive tone.

"Oh my goodness! Yes, doctor?"

"Please tell me that there are not four vials of blood missing. Tell me I'm wrong!"

"Well, they're not where they are supposed to be. I called **Nurse Jackie** because she was on duty at the time and she said they should have been there."

"So… that's it? No one knows anything else? Let me explain something to you; that blood was from John James. He's the producer that made the Black Butterfly soap opera that's so popular and countless other hit shows. The guy's a legend in the entertainment world! He's also been diagnosed as HIV positive."

"I understand that, sir, but I don't know where else to look. Do you have any suggestions?"

"My suggestion is that you find them. He wants to keep his condition confidential and that blood is a major health hazard. We can't just take more blood from the man and move on!"

"I understand … I will get right on it. I'll go back to the lab and ask around."

"Please do. I don't want that blood to end up in the wrong hands. It was taken in vacuum tubes, right?"

"Yes sir," the nurse responded.

"You know what that means; don't you?"

"Yes, it means that **the virus** can live for up to **seven days** in those tubes."

"Correct Nurse Mary… so get on it!"

Meanwhile… John was in his room falling asleep, but still mumbling his complaints. When suddenly, the hallway door slowly creaked open with little to no sound and a shadowy figure stood over John's bed clutching two needles.

Slightly awakened; John barked, "Damn nurse, didn't I say no more needles…"

In an instant, a knee slammed onto the back of his neck and the needles quickly sank deep into his ass cheeks before being broken off. John tried to scream, but his frail hundred and thirty-eight pound frame could barely lift off of the bed.

John's arms swung wildly as he searched for the nurse's call button, but his head kept sinking deeper and deeper into his pillow the more he struggled. As his vision blurred, John began to choke and lose consciousness. But before he blacked out, the pressure was suddenly released and all John saw was the shadowy figure exiting the room.

"Somebody help me! Help-p-p!"

DAY ONE:

AQUAINTANCES

Wednesday

BLACK BUTTERFLY 2 by FEENIX

Chapter I: WIZ & GUNZ

It was a normal Wednesday in Baltimore with the exception that schools had a half day. Nadet' looked forward to eating his Butter Crunch cookies and hanging out with his two best friends; Ricky and Dion, or Dee as most people liked to call him. The afternoon was bright and sunny when Nadet' exited the school building while Ricky and Dee waited for him at the bottom of the steps.

"Yo, what's up Birthday Boy! What you gettin' into this afternoon? Cuz I'm tryin' to get something to eat at Micky-Dees, son-son!" Dee rubbed his stomach as he played with the toothpick hanging out of his mouth.

"Man, my birthday was a week ago; where have you been?" Nadet shook his head briefly then continued, "I gotta go to Fells Point to get a City Paper. After that, it's whateva as far as I'm concerned. But I do gotta holla at my grandmother if we gonna be out for a long time though." Nadet was very anxious to get to the next destination and get the City Paper.

"Sound Garden again? What's up with you and the City Paper all the time? Every Wednesday you act like a new Tupac joint came out or something. You know what I'm sayin' R," responded Dee as he laughed and slapped five with Ricky.

"Yo, I'm not even trippin' because I want to go to Sound Garden anyway and get some more soul joints. You know I like Earth, Wind, & Fire and all that old shit. I'm an old soul, son-son," Ricky interjected.

"Whatever you say... as long as there's some bitches down there, I'm straight. You know they call me Dee-Nice the pimp, right?"

"Alright old soul and pimp Dee-Nice, let's make tracks," Nadet' said as he laughed at his friends.

Once they arrived downtown at Fells Point, Ricky and Dion saw a guy named Chucky they both knew from juvenile hall. He was wearing a thick link chain, a diamond faced watch, and all new gear that looked like he just pulled the tags off of them. It seemed that no one found it strange but Nadet' that a kid their age had all that kind of stuff. Chucky was extremely loud and flashy. He went out of his way to make everyone think he was hardcore and had a sneaky smile that made Nadet's skin crawl.

Nadet' decided to cut the introduction and conversation short so he continued to Sound Garden and left them there to talk. Dudes like Chucky rubbed him the wrong way while Ricky and Dee seemed to understand them better.

"Yo, my niggas, what's good? I ain't seen ya'll since I was in Juvie," said Chucky.

"I know boy, but I see you shinin' like the sun. What's up with the gear and all dem jewels," asked Dee.

"Ain't nothing you can't do, Dog. My man's and 'em put me on and now I'm tryin' to build my team. So, what up?"

"Shit... you know I like the money but cookin, baggin, and sellin just ain't my thing," responded Dee.

"I know that, but I also know you ain't scared to bang that thang on niggas, too. That's why I wanted to have you as my enforcer. I can get you every type of gun you ever wanted. I know you like that," said Chucky.

"Damn, that's what I'm talkin' about. I can definitely handle that, but if I'm around-niggas in B-more ain't gonna fuck with you anyway. Trust me, I already got most of these niggas shook." Dion laughed before Ricky interrupted him.

"Man... all that thrill seeker, tough guy shit you can have. I'm only concerned with the paper. How much paper can we get with you, Chucky... because we all know the consequences of this shit," interjected Ricky.

"I knew you would say that Ricky, that's why I want you to use your connections to set-up some deals. Since you know everybody from prep niggas to thug motherfuckers, it should come easy. We can make an unlimited amount of doe, Fam."

Meanwhile... Nadet' was in Sound Garden listening to a meditation CD on the store headphones and reading the personal ad section of the City Paper. He found what he was looking for, highlighted it, and then kept reading it over and over again for comprehension.

I call you sun because you shine like one. In the garden, one sees the sun many times. But in seven days I plan to sea the sunrise. All because natural things have family ties... like the sun, mother earth, and sibling butterflies. Why oh why did the butterfly convert time to 180 degrees of nine?

"Yo, space cadet number one!" Dee grabbed one head phone and let it flop against Nadet's head.

"Stop playing, Asshole! I'm doing something real serious over here," said Nadet' angrily.

"Dayum... my fault man, but me and Ricky been callin' you for a minute. When you're reading the City Paper it's like you zone out! What's the deal," asked Dee.

"Man, ya'll wouldn't understand even if I tried to explain. Let's just say I'm trying to figure something out and I'm not in a playing mood right now, okay?"

"We understand, Nadet'. Don't pay attention to Dee. Look, I found that Sam Cooke CD I was lookin for," said Ricky.

"I was bor-n-n by the river!" Dee interrupted with his usual antics, singing the first line of Sam Cooke's song.

"Well, at least you know something that's not guns and all that bang-bang shoot'em up shit." Ricky shook his head and laughed at Dee.

Though both Ricky and Dee were street dudes and childhood friends, but they were drastically different. Dee was wild; he loved fast girls, cars, clothes, and excitement. He was the typical personality that would gravitate toward drug dealing. Dee's major problem was his infatuation with guns and the fact that he possessed an inner anger aimed at the world. He loved Nadet' because he saw him as the kind of dude he wanted to be; extremely smart, charismatic, artsy, and ambitious.

Ricky, on the other hand, was fundamentally different. He appeared calm; though he loved all the things Dee loved, he mastered control. Ricky hated what he thought his life would be if things stayed the same and blamed everyone for his problems but himself. He was the type of guy other dudes loved and pledged allegiance to. A great manipulator of people, Ricky would flip on you at a moment's notice. He loved Nadet' also because he admired him in his own way. Ricky knew the real Nadet' to be pure of heart and strong of mind, even though he appeared to be shy and easy going. Ricky could see that Nadet' was extremely calculating and would commit to what ever he set his mind to.

"Yo, ya'll niggas pay for that shit and let's go. I want to talk to you about something, Day-Day," said Dee.

"Oh no, here we go again... what is it? I know it's something I'm not gonna like, so tell me now," replied Nadet'.

"Shut up, Dee. Wait until we get outside before you tell 'em," interrupted Ricky.

"Tell me what? Now ya'll niggas are startin' to scare me."

Nadet' and Ricky paid for their CD's as the boys exited the store. Ricky bought Sam Cooke's greatest hits while Nadet' bought an Asian meditation CD. The kind that had sounds of running water, birds, and babbling brooks set to a harp playing in the background. The boys walked to a restaurant where the owner was cool and let them play pool in the back. Tension grew thick as Nadet' waited for Ricky and Dee to tell him the big news. He figured it was something that had to do with Chucky and that wasn't good.

"Yo, we got a way to get some real money and it ain't even hard," said Dee.

Nadet' laughed to himself because he felt like he was about to be sold something by an extremely bad salesman. "Ain't even hard, huh Dee? Well... I'm listening."

"Yo, my man Chucky is caked up and killin' it out here in the streets. He wants us to come in with him, and check this out... we don't even have to sell nothing." Dee sounded like the boy who just bought three magic beans in a fairy tale.

"Oh, yeah? Sounds like a hell of a deal so far," sarcastically said Nadet'. "Either you're that dumb or you just don't think things through."

Ricky jumped into the conversation, "Man, all Dee is trying to say is that Chucky got a dope hook up and he want us to be his team. Hear us out on this, man..."

"Ricky, you can't be down with this too? We already know that hustlin' somehow never works out... because the police know all the angles. Do you really think that Chucky is smart enough to beat the odds and get ya'll paid? You better think hard before you do anything because both of you have got priors, remember dat!"

"You're right Nadet', that's why we want you to come with us. He wants me for my connections and Dee as an enforcer. That's what Dee meant by we don't have to sell anything to get paid."

"So Chucky must be the brains of this operation, huh? Don't make me laugh... ain't nothing about him that says intelligence to me. Good luck because I'm definitely not down."

"I told him we wasn't gonna do it unless you came in with us, so would you at least think about it? It's goin down around eleven o'clock."

"There's nothing to think about Rick, I've got enough problems."

"Aight then, stay up my nigga. If you change your mind, holla at us."

Ricky and Dee went their separate way and Nadet' headed home. He kept reading the personal ad in the City Paper over and over again in an attempt to figure out what it meant.

I call you sun because you shine like one. In the garden, one sees the sun many times. But in seven days I plan to sea the sunrise. All because natural things have family ties... like the sun, mother earth, and sibling butterflies. Why oh why did the butterfly convert time to 180 degrees of nine?

Chapter **II**: Agent JC the FED

"First off... I'd like to say congrats JC, for being appointed as head of the FUOCI of the FBI," said Matt, one of JC's colleagues at the Bureau.

"Wow! That sure was a mouthful of alphabet soup, Matt. At least now we know you made it through grade school," responded Agent JC as he chuckled.

"Yeah right, well at least we can look forward to some excitement around here now that the self proclaimed 007 has this division."

"Oh you're funny, but it's not self proclaimed at all, Matt... your momma gave me that title!"

"At any rate, this one should be a good first for you... the Ms. Machiavelli case! Here's the local police file for Eboni Edwards, real name Eboni Burton."

"Eboni Edwards, the girl from the soap opera? My wife use to record it all the time, it was one of her favorite shows," said JC.

"Good, so you're remotely familiar with the show but are you familiar with the case?"

"Vaguely, so why don't you fill me in because I'm dying to know what makes this a FBI case?"

"Well, first she was accused of murdering the wife of the show's producer. Then she went on some type of rampage claiming she didn't do it, until finally she was killed by driving a car into a solid brick wall."

"Case closed, right?" Agent JC jokingly smiled and threw his hands in the air because he knew there was more to the story.

"Wrong, it was reported by the news that she was dead and the family even had a memorial funeral, but the body found at the scene was not hers. Though it was badly charred with busted teeth, BCPD still figured it out."

"So now we have a case... but what makes it federal?"

"We think she's networking across state lines and is affiliated with both the NOI and the Black Guerilla Syndicate. I know it doesn't make much sense, but shit... there are so many holes in this case that the local police might even be involved. It's all there, look at the report."

"Wow, sounds like a soap opera if I ever of heard one. The only thing missing is money."

"Wrong again. Madeline, the producer's wife, was worth well over a hundred million dollars that she inherited. It's a viable theory that the girl was framed so the producer could get his wife's fortune."

"Wow, I had no idea. That's interesting, so let's start with the family or any relatives. I'll read the file today but I want surveillance on them now."

"She has a mother, sister, and young son she used to take care of. I think that it would be hard for her to totally walk away from them."

"I agree. It says in her file that she was represented by council; get someone on him too. Make sure they stay out of sight; we need to collect our own data before drawing any conclusions. It's obvious the original investigations are going to be worthless to me."

Agent JC was very ambitious and had spent his whole life in some form of law enforcement. After studying criminal justice at Morgan State University, he worked at parole and probation for many years before making it to the Federal Bureau of Investigations. Based on his outstanding record, the FEDs made him the head of a new Federal Urban Organized Crime Initiative. His first case under this new initiative was Eboni's... which the FEDs labeled, **Ms. Machiavelli**.

Being a native of Baltimore, Maryland himself, agent JC was extremely familiar with the city.

His ambitions of going all the way to the top served as motivation for him. The Eboni Edwards case was high profile because of the people involved and amount of local media coverage it had already received. Plus, factoring in a fake death and possible cover up gave it the potential to go much deeper and make national news. It was definitely the type of case that whole careers were built on.

Agent JC hurried to set everything in motion. Scheduled an interview with the local investigating officer, set up surveillance schedules, compiling background intel on immediate family members, and briefing his team. By seven o'clock that same evening, everything was in place.

BLACK BUTTERFLY 2 by FEENIX

Chapter III: Drake

"Yes, I'm waiting for him to come out now. Don't worry; I'll whip him into shape. He will definitely be ready for court. We've filed all the papers and everything is set to go on the legal end. Over the next few days, I'll make sure he knows what to say," said Mr. Greenberg, John's lawyer.

Mr. Greenberg called John to tell him that Drake was being picked up from jail. Drake was Eboni's ex-husband and Nadet's biological father. He served time at Jessup correctional facility for parole violation and Mr. Greenberg simply didn't like him because he thought Drake was low class trash. It was like torture for Mr. Greenberg to deal with Drake but like John said… they had a job to do.

John and Mr. Greenberg contacted Drake as soon as they found out about his existence and the fact that his sentence was almost over. They gave legal and financial support to him in exchange for help with a plan they had once he got out of jail.

Drake himself; was an ill-tempered asshole that used to beat Eboni and practically every woman he was ever involved with. He liked to "put the big hand down," as he always said, when a chick needed a little discipline. His six four muscular frame made him both attractive to women and intimidating to men. Drake's bad temper and violent outbursts had gotten him in trouble with the law his whole life, so jail was no big deal to him.

"What's crackin', Greenberg? How ya livin?" Drake remarked as the driver opened the limo door to let him in.

"What -is -cracking? Oh, I can see that this is going to be a long freakin' ride, Convict." Mr. Greenberg replied.

"I know it's tough for you, dealing with a real man and all… but try."

"A real man? Where? All I see is an oversized little boy who likes to throw tantrums when he doesn't get his way. So let's stick to the script and cut the idle conversation, okay? We have a job to do, so let's do it then part ways richer and happier."

"Cool, Berg Man..." responded Drake as he continued to piss Mr. Greenberg off.

"Whatever... it's useless talking to you. When we get to the office, I'm going to go over everything you need to say in court-word for word."

The limo pulled up in front of Mr. Greenberg's office. His whole staff was still working at eight o'clock that night like it was mid afternoon. Drake walked in with his black sweat suit and fisherman hat draped over his eyes. Everyone stopped moving in the office like Mr. Greenberg had walked in with Hannibal Lector. Greenberg shut his office door behind him and told the secretary to hold all his calls.

"Okay Drake, here's the skinny... both we and the police now know that your little pain in the ass wife is not dead..." said Mr. Greenberg.

"Ex-wife! Get it right," Drake interrupted.

"Ex-wife, my mistake... I won't waste time re-explaining the things we've already briefed you on. Instead, I'll bring you up to date. The body originally thought to be Eboni's in the crash was that of Sharon Jackson, the other security guard at our studio."

"Oh shit, you mean... she killed her too?"

"Yes. The police never identified the body as Eboni because they could hardly identify it as a human it was so badly charred. She must have dowsed the inside of the whole car with gasoline that dried in the carpet and seats. When the car hit that wall both Sharon and Jada were already dead. The gas tank was already filled to capacity and Eboni had set the back seat on fire when she pulled off. I mean the car was a fucking bomb!"

"Day-um, you know she got that toughness from being around me so long. I used to whip that ass from time to time just to keep her in line. The bitch definitely needed some discipline because she can get rowdy."

"That's why we need you because you know her. John doesn't want to under-estimate her again. Last time we wanted her to go to jail for Madeline's murder but this time we need her dead. Can you handle that? Will you be able to kill the mother of your child... when the time comes?"

"Most men will never admit it but that's the easiest person in the world to kill. Statistics prove that everyday. When a woman is murdered... nine times out of ten, it's her ex-lover, boyfriend, or husband. Plus, I got an old score to settle with that bitch, so my answer to that is absolutely!"

"Okay then... but stick to the plan. I have to get you ready for court on Friday. We have a barber and tailor here right now that are going to make you look like a pillar of society. I'm going to get everything ready for you because there's a lot to go over before you will be ready to see the judge."

Mr. Greenberg exited the office while the barber and tailor went to work on Drake. He didn't want to waste anytime because he knew it wasn't going to be easy to pass Drake off as a likable guy. After Mr. Greenberg gathered the information from his legal research team, he re-entered the office and saw that Drake's face was cleanly shaven.

"Wow, where did Drake go? Excuse me, Sir, but have you seen a broken down jail bird named Drake around here," John sarcastically asked Drake.

"Why don't you stand on a chair and say that because I can't hear your short ass from way down there," responded Drake.

"I'll tell ya what... let me stand on my wallet then I'll definitely be talking over your head!"

"You know something, Greenberg... you're pretty funny for an old gay Jew. They should call you Ben Gay-berg," Drake laughed hysterically by himself as everyone in the room got silent.

The insults the two men hurled at each other lightened the mood but always escalated out of control. Mr. Greenberg somehow always managed to maintain his composure in the end. After the tailor took Drake's measurements, Greenberg stirred the conversation back to the business at hand.

"Okay, play time is over, let's start prepping you for Friday's court appearance. The overall plan is to draw her out of hiding. We know she would never leave her family so she still has to be around," said Mr. Greenberg.

"Where's John," asked Drake.

"He won't be released from the hospital until tomorrow. Can you please focus; we have a lot to go over. Friday is right around the corner."

"Alright, I got you. You don't have to talk to me like I'm stupid. You want me to ask for visitation with my son... that's why ya'll paid my back child support, right? Then hopefully, she'll come out of hiding to stop my first visit."

"That's the first part, but like I said earlier... we are done with under-estimating her. We've set up some accounts for you so it looks like you're well-off due to some wise investing while you were gone."

"Aight, so now the big question... what am I getting paid?"

"Like I said, we put some money in a few accounts for you..."

"Man, that's just fun money... living expenses. I'm talking about some shit that I will never have to work again in my life. The type of money that John got from his wife's inheritance! Ah ha... you didn't think I knew about that."

"It doesn't matter to me if you know. The beauty of the whole plan is the fact that you will determine your own pay, Drake."

"Huh," replied Drake.

"We made sure that the local police ruled her death an accident... they're in our back pocket. Only we know that she is still alive. John then pulled some strings at Eboni's insurance company so the boy would receive a huge payout!"

"Oh I get it now... if I get custody of my son then the insurance money is mine. Eboni definitely won't have that shit... s-o she'll come out of hiding to stop me and then we take her out."

"N-o, not we, Drake... you!" Mr. Greenburg laughed with a sinister smile.

"Then, my ass goes right back to jail, motherfucker! What kinda plan is that?"

"The perfect plan... because how can you go to jail for killing someone that's already been declared dead? All we have to do is help keep her secret and get rid of the body when it's done. No one is looking for her!"

"Damn, that's some cold shit... but brilliant! Maybe I can even have a little fun before I lower the boom on her ass."

Chapter **IV**: Best Friend

After Eboni faked her own death, she went to live with her best friend and old college roommate… Patsy. She was a mild mannered, loyal, and trustworthy friend to Eboni. They called themselves Siamese twins in school because they claimed to be able to feel each other's pain. When Eboni was accused of murdering Madeline James she called Patsy first. Patsy would send money to Eboni anytime she needed it and was always available to help.

Patsy married a basketball player named Zeus Cartwright from the Washington Wizards a year before Eboni landed her role on the Black Butterfly soap opera. Both Zeus and Patsy rushed into marriage because she was pregnant at the time. She later lost the baby due to some "mysterious" complications, a situation that never set quite right with Eboni. In spite of the tragic ordeal, Patsy insisted that they never had any marital problems and always spoke as if things were picture perfect.

Though Patsy was often home alone for weeks at a time because of Zeus' schedule, he still had a strong presence in the house. Everything had to be neat, clean, and perfect at all times. Patsy walked around her own home like she wasn't comfortable and appeared nervous about anything being out of the norm. Eboni often wondered what was really going on behind closed doors because she could sense that her best friend wasn't happy.

"Patty-cake, is Zeus still coming home this weekend," asked Eboni.

"Yea, my baby will be home for a few days. I'm gonna buy a nice bottle of wine and cook something special, then hopefully I can get some," replied Patsy.

Once again Pasty was making everything sound too perfect for Eboni's comfort. While staying there, she noticed a few things around the home that were out of the ordinary so Eboni decided to pick Patsy's brain.

"Ya'll must be in to some kinky stuff because all I see is gauze and compresses around here."

"Girl, he's an athlete, something is always hurting on that man."

"Looks like you are pretty accident prone yourself. Your arm just healed, right?"

"Yea, I'm good. I don't want you worrying about me when you have so much going on yourself."

"I know, but you've been here for me with all of what I'm up against. I want to let you know that I'm here for you, too."

"Thanks, Eboni. Are you making any headway with your case?"

"Yeah, I guess. John checked into the hospital where my sister, Jackie, worked. She let me in and I got some valuable information that could help."

"Whoa! I can't believe that he was there. What kind of information did you get?"

"Well, when Madeline came to my trailer to confront me about an affair with John, she threw some papers in my face. The chick was mad as hell and kept yelling all types of shit before I could tell her it wasn't true. Then Madeline clocked me in my grill piece! After I whipped her ass... I took the papers along with my things and left. I never read them until recently."

"So what did they say?" asked Patsy.

"It appeared that Madeline found out she was HIV positive... and since she thought that John was having an affair with me..."

"She thought that you gave it to him, then he to her," added Patsy as she finished Eboni's sentence.

"Yep! It seemed that everybody knew John was gay but her, that's why she was so off the hook that day. Anyway… when my sister told me that John checked in I went there to get confirmation that he had HIV so I could link everything together for my defense."

"So did you get anything that said he had HIV like his wife?"

"Nope, they hadn't tested the blood yet so I took it."

"You took his blood! Why on earth would you do that? Yuck…," squeaked Patsy.

"Girl, the blood was in vacuum tubes. It's good for up to seven days like that, so I figured I'd get it tested myself."

Later that night… Nadet' sat at home with his grandmother and his aunt Jackie trying not to look at the clock. He had a bad feeling in the pit of his stomach about Rickyy and Dee's eleven o'clock meeting with Chucky. At about ten thirty, Rickyy called Nadet' on his cell phone.

"Yo, Day-Day! What's the deal, son? We are on our way to get up with Chucky. This is your last chance to get down with us."

"Nah, I'm straight. To be honest…" Nadet' paused because he heard Dee in the background talking to someone. He asked, "Are ya'll there already, Rickyy? Who's that I hear in the background?"

"No, we're not there yet. That's just Dee and Black Rob."

Black Rob was a twenty-two year old hustler from the neighborhood that built a notorious reputation of being a killer. He had been in and out of jail his whole teenage life and it was rumored that he had killed as many as eight people.

Dee looked up too this dude because he didn't answer to anyone and no one ever played with his money. People feared Black Rob so much that they would come looking for him just to pay up.

"Black Rob? What is he doing there?"

"Oh, Chucky said that he needed to re-up real quick until his connect came through with another package. Me and Dee knew Rob always stayed stocked so we figured we'd hook him up with Chucky."

Nadet's gut feeling was finally confirmed. The type of dude Black Rob was and the type of dude Chucky seemed to be would not mix well in Nadet's opinion. Rickyy and Dee, his two best friends, were about to put themselves right in the middle of something bad.

"I wish ya'll wouldn't do this shit tonight. My stomach has been hurting every since we parted ways."

"Don't start with that hocus-pocus shit, man. We are okay and we about to get paid, ya heard me! I gotta go, he's here now. I'll text you later to let you know how it went down. Don't worry so much."

DAY TWO:

"Differences"

Thursday

BLACK BUTTERFLY 2 by FEENIX

Chapter **V**: Home

The next morning around nine o'clock, Nadet' woke up and saw that Rickyy and Dee did not call him as promised. It was still early so he figured that they were probably still asleep. Nadet' grabbed the city paper and walked into the kitchen. As he made himself a bowl of Apple Jacks, Nadet' kept reading the personal ad in the City Paper.

Since his mother's self staged death, Nadet' kept in contact with her via personal ads in the City Paper. Eboni would submit them over the internet in the form of poetry so that Nadet' could decode them later. The ads were free and Nadet' could respond the same way without worrying about the police. Every Wednesday, when the new City Paper would come out, he'd hurry to Sound Garden to get it. However, yesterday's poem was definitely different. It was coded very hard and more difficult for him to interpret, so he knew that it had to be an extremely important message.

"We're home!" yelled Nadet's Aunt Jackie as she came through the door with his grandmother hanging on her shoulder.

"Hey, Aunt Jackie, when did ya'll leave? I thought you were still in your rooms asleep."

"No, Mama had a doctor's appointment this morning so we left early."

"Okay, so how'd it go?"

"Let me walk Mama up stairs and I'll be down to talk to you, okay?"

Nadet' nodded his head yes but felt instantly concerned. His grandmother didn't say anything to him when she walked in and his aunt seemed like she was attempting to stay upbeat. At that point in his life, he had gotten so much bad news it was easy for him to tell when there was something wrong.

After helping her mother to bed, Jackie came back to the kitchen and sat beside Nadet'. He

hated the big build up of tension and wished that she
would just say what ever she had to say.

"Day, Day… What are you doing?"

"Reading the City Paper and waiting for
you to stop stalling and tell me what's up."

"Well, Mr. Smart Ass… Mama is going
blind. How's that for what's up?"

Jackie snapped at Nadet' because she
was already feeling bad from hearing the news. She
put her head down and started crying. Nadet's heart
dropped and he felt bad for not being more patient
with his aunt. He never saw Jackie cry before so he
knew that she was deeply hurt.

"I'm sorry, Aunt Jackie. I didn't mean to
sound all insensitive and things but.…"

"It's okay Day-Day, you don't have to
apologize. I'm in a messed up state of mind right
now. I could tell Mama was scared, I mean really
scared… when the doctor broke the news to us. "

"Is there anything we can do? What did the doctor say exactly?"

"Well, it's called retinopathy and it is treatable. The main factor is time; Mama has had diabetes for almost 8 years now. She needed to have her eyes checked every year, but she didn't. The doctor said early detection of the condition is essential. He hopes that we caught it in time but he's not sure. All we can do now is closely monitor Mama's blood sugar level because she has not been doing a good job. Everything that went on with your mom and Betty depressed her so she obviously started neglecting herself."

"Why don't we tell Grandma Rose that my mother is still alive?"

"That would help in one way but hurt in so many others. Plus, your mother said not to until she decided to reveal herself."

"She did? When did you hear from her?"

"I helped her get some information from the hospital a little while ago."

"So, you saw her?"

"No, she emailed me and I arranged everything. She had came and gone before I even knew what happened. So, why won't you tell me how you stay in contact with her?"

"She told me not to. My mom said that the less people who know, the more protected they are."

"Okay, but you know that your mom's lawyer is coming over here to meet with us this afternoon."

"Mr. Muhammad? Is it about insurance?"

"No, the insurance company is not contesting the accidental death claim. They are going to give us the big payout. However, we recently got a letter from another lawyer stating that your father wanted visitation rights."

"My father? Where did he come from? Never mind; I know where he came from…jail, but I didn't know he was out."

"Yes, he did get out recently and Mr. Muhammad says that he's doing pretty well for himself. How do you feel about that? You know…possibly seeing him on a regular basis."

"I don't know how I feel…"

Suddenly Nadet' was interrupted by the doorbell. Jackie went to answer the door as Nadet' took his City Paper to the living room and sat it on the table in front of him. The paper was all marked up and highlighted where he constantly tried to crack his mother's code. No one other than Jackie and he knew his mother was still alive, not even Mr. Muhammad.

When Jackie answered the door, it was Mr. Muhammad as suspected. Both he and Jackie stood near the door whispering as Nadet' observed. It was obvious that they were talking about him and Nadet' hated that.

"What's going on Day-Day?" Mr. Muhammad playfully asked.

"Call me Nadet'. So my father finally decided to show up after all these years, huh?"

Mr. Muhammad looked at Jackie before answering Nadet' and said, "Oka-y, straight to business I see. I'm afraid it's a little more than that Nadet'. Yes, your father is now requesting visitation but he's also paid off all his arrears in child support."

"Mo' money, mo' money! That's good, right? I don't have a problem seeing him. So everything is everything?"

"I don't know Nadet'. I have some suspicions that I will keep to myself for now. Oh, I saw your two buddies, Ricky and Dion, this morning."

"Where?" anxiously asked Nadet'.

"At a bail hearing this morning... They got picked up on some drug charges last night with another guy. Thanks to me they were released on their own recognizes to their parents but the other guy wasn't a juvenile and had priors so they set a high bail for him."

"So, only one other guy was locked up with them?" asked Nadet'.

"Yes... I don't know the details of the case yet, but the other guy was Robert Jarrod Blackmon."

Black Rob... aw shit! Nadet' thought to himself as his eyes widened and darted upstairs before Mr. Muhammad could finish talking.

"Wait a minute, Nadet'! Don't you want to hear about you insurance payout?"

"Tell Aunt Jackie the rest; I'm cool with whatever she wants."

"Well, Jackie, he is about to be a very rich little boy..."

After Nadet' ran upstairs he grabbed his cell and immediately called Ricky. He wanted to know everything that happened because he already felt that things were going to go bad.

"Hello," Ricky answered the phone but he was whispering.

"Yo, what is going on? I just talked to Mr. Muhammad... what happened?"

"Ma-n, my peeps are trippin' right now, so I can't talk. I need to see you though. Meet me at Seven-Eleven near your house. I'm gonna sneak out!"

"Alright, I'll be there in like fifteen minutes. Are you okay?"

"I'm cool... see you in a minute," said Ricky before he hung up the phone.

Nadet' put his boots on and grabbed his coat before running out the front door. He didn't bother to stop as Jackie and Mr. Muhammad yelled to him from the kitchen to wait a minute. With a light jog, Nadet' arrived at the Seven-Eleven. He sat on the curb with his hood over his head and bobbed to music in his head.

A few minutes later, Ricky came from behind the building with his hood and hat on. He looked worried and asked Nadet' to walk with him. Ricky kept shaking his head in a slow side to side motion.

"Yo, we fucked up. I mean, we r-eally fucked up... we shoulda listened to you and that stomach of yours."

"Ricky, what's the deal? How did ya'll fuck up, man?"

"Well, for one thing... Chucky set us up. He wasn't even there when we arrived. Rob brought a

60

lot of shit with him because of how Dee hyped everything up."

"So, what happened?"

"While we were waiting for Chucky, he kept calling Dee and saying he was only a few minutes away. Rob kept asking us questions we couldn't answer so I told him to wait for Chuck. Then before we knew it, bam! The police were everywhere; lights in our faces, guns drawn, dogs... da whole nine!"

"Oh shit! What did ya'll do?"

"We got on the fuckin' ground! They came out like we were Columbian drug lords or something. The worst part was the way Black Rob looked at me and Dee. He just stared without saying a word, and then he turned away and wouldn't look at us at all. We all know what that means..."

"Damn, he's gonna think ya'll set him up," replied Nadet.

"But we didn't, it was Chucky that..."

"There is no Chucky! Rob never saw him so he doesn't exist... you get it? As far as Black Rob is concerned; you and Dee set him up from jump street."

"But we got locked up with him, so how could he still think that we..."

"Easy, you're out and he's not! No bail... no nothing, you're free as a bird. How do you think that looks? Man, ya'll better get low because when he gets out it's gonna get ugly."

"Shit... this is fucked up! What are we gonna do, Day-Day?"

"I told you man... damn! Ya'll don't fuckin' listen. You and Dee got all the tools but not the plan," yelled Nadet. "Fuck it... get Dee on the phone so we can get together and prepare for Rob's release. Plus, I wanna get bitch ass Chucky!"

Ricky called Dee on his cell phone and told him where they were going to meet up. Nadet' and Ricky caught the bus to the north side of Baltimore and met Dee at Mount Pleasant Golf Course. Nadet' led them into the wooded area, down a trail along the side of the course. At the bottom was a creek that had a highway on the other side. It was a very secluded area. Dee and Ricky looked around in awe.

"Damn, what is this? I feel like I'm somewhere far away from Baltimore..." said Dee.

"Yeah, this is cool as a mug, Day-Day. I can get with this," added Ricky.

"This is a place my mom use to bring me sometimes. I would skip rocks over the water while she worked on her poetry. She knew about tons of places like this. I remember one poem she wrote called *Fight*."

"So what's up... you gonna give us some or not?"

"If you don't ever fight, you'll never soar to higher heights. You'll be doomed to fall and never conquer the tight ropes of life. Hope lives on the other side of strife, like the smooth edge on the other side of a Samurai's knife. Fight, fight, fight…"

"Whoa! That's hot. Is there more?"

"Yeah, but that's not what we're here for. I've got so much on me right now that all I want to do is handle these niggas and move on. It's time to give ya'll something you never had before… a plan. We will crush anything Rob throws at us and handle that snitch ass friend of yours too."

Chapter **VI**: The Visitor

Ding... Dong!

The doorbell sounded as Jackie and her mother mixed their favorite dish together in a pot... corned beef and cabbage. They weren't expecting anyone, so Jackie anxiously went to see who their lunch time visitor was. She wiped her hands on her apron as she opened the interior door.

"Oh, my God... Drake?" Jackie couldn't believe her eyes. Drake was standing at the door smiling in a dark blue business suit.

"What's up, Jackie- Jack? Long time no-see, can I come in for a minute?"

"Nadet's not here...," replied Jackie. She was so stunned he was there that she didn't know what to say.

"That's okay; I was kinda hoping that we could talk before we go to court. I think it would be beneficial for all parties involved."

Jackie paused for a moment. She remembered what Mr. Muhammad said about Drake possibly having other motives so she let him in. Jackie wanted to pick his brain and see what angle he was coming from.

"Come on in Drake. You sure look nice. I have never known you to wear suits."

"Yeah, well I'm a new man so you're going to see a lot more of that." Drake stepped inside, looked around, and made his way over to the living room couch. "The place looks nice; ya'll changed things around."

Grandma Rose heard Drake's voice and tried to make her way into the living room. She bumped into the dinning room table because of her blurred vision before Jackie could help her.

"Mama, watch your step! Let me come and get you if you need to go anywhere."

It really bothered Grandma Rose that she now had to depend on other people so much. She no longer felt like the strong matriarch of the family. Though her body was showing signs of age her mental was still sharp so she insisted on sitting in on the conversation with Drake.

"Hey, Ms. Rose. Are you okay?" asked Drake.

"I'm fine. State your business Drake because we know you want something."

"Whoa, Ms. Rose. What's with all the hostility? I'm here on a peaceful mission, trying to see if we can reach some kind of agreement before we step into the courtroom… that's all."

"Mama, let me handle it… I got this," whispered Jackie. "Drake, I'm sorry. Mama is just a little protective; we want to hear what you've got to say."

"Alright, I won't make it long. I'm doing quite well for myself now. I've got a new start on life… job, money, and the whole nine. I'm in the process of looking for homes, as we speak."

"That's very good Drake. We're glad that you are turning your life around but the question is…"

"Why am I here?" Drake finished Jackie's sentence. "I'm here because I would like my son to be a part of my new life."

"In what way, Drake? How do we achieve him, quote unquote, being a part of your new life? Can you be more specific?"

"Well… seeing that his mom has passed away and all, I think he should be with me. I want shared custody."

"Bingo! I told you he was up to no good," shouted Grandma Rose.

"If we can't agree on shared custody before court, I'm going for full custody! So what do you think?"

"I think you better get the fuck out of my house! You don't come up in here with ultimatums after all these years. Me, Mama, and my sisters took care of that boy... not you. Now, I'm not gonna tell you again... get the fuck out before I start movin' some furniture up in here!"

"Well, I tried to make this easy but you can't be nice to niggas. Tha-t's right, I said niggas! So, get ready for a fight bitch, because I got the money and time to take this all the way!"

Grandma Rose grabbed Jackie before she could swing at Drake. He didn't flinch at all; he just stood there smiling devilishly as he stared both of them down. He pulled out a card and threw it at them.

"Here's my number, use it!"

After a moment, Drake shook his head like he was disgusted and finally walked out. Grandma Rose released Jackie and sat back in her chair.

"Well, well, well… Miss-I-got–this. What are we going to do now?" asked Grandma Rose.

"I don't know. Somehow we have to get word to Eboni. She would know what to do but the e-mail account was cancelled two days ago. Nadet' is gonna have to tell us how he contacted her."

"Where is Day-Day?" asked Grandma.

"I don't know exactly where he is Mama. He was going to meet up with his friends so they're probably hanging at the mall or something. He'll be home when he's supposed to."

"Jackie, I told you to keep a tighter grip on him, especially with everything he's been through."

"Ma, he's a teenage boy. I think keeping him cooped up in the house is the last thing we should do. Let him go out and have a little life of his own. It will help him cope better."

"Is that your professional opinion...Dr. Jackie? I mean, you must be some type of doctor if you think you know more than me with over 50 years of raising children. Huh?"

"I'm not saying that Mama, you taking this the wrong way. All I meant was..."

"You meant nothing! Go find that boy and bring him here... now!"

"Okay Mama."

BLACK BUTTERFLY 2 by FEENIX

Chapter VII: The Hit

"We are trying to find the subject. His friends have been acquired in front of the Seven Eleven… hopefully he'll be along soon."

Around 8:00pm, agents working under JC had lost track of Nadet' so they decided to keep his friends under surveillance until he showed up. Both Ricky and Dee stood in Seven Eleven's parking lot, slap boxing the night away on Baltimore's rugged eastside. The agents didn't know what was going on but it appeared they were waiting for someone.

"Yo… there's a black car over there on the corner, just chillin" said Ricky.

"Where?" asked Dee.

"Don't look now, but it seems like they're on a mission."

"You think that's him?"

"I don't know, but be ready for anything. If shit goes down it will be fast and furious!"

At that moment, the agents observed a male with a chocolate hooded sweat shirt and blue jeans approach the boys from behind. They could not identify the person because he had the hood over his head. However, the agents were sure it was not Nadet' because the person was too tall. They continued to observe.

"Yo, little niggas…what's up?" said the hooded male.

Ricky and Dee were startled; they turned around quickly but did not reply. Ricky immediately looked at the guy's hands and waist for a gun while Dee broke his mug down.

"Black Rob sent me to tell you that he ain't got no rap for ya'll so stop calling him. He also wanted me to tell you that ya'll some snitch ass bitches!"

"Wait a minute, we didn't know…"

"Fuck what ya'll knew! I should take care of this shit right here, right now!"

The guy grabbed Dee and his sweat shirt lifted to reveal a black nine millimeter handgun in his waist. Ricky grabbed the gun from Dee's waistline and clicked the safety off as he ran his shoulder into the guy knocking off of Dee.

"Check this out… Rob ain't gonna believe shit we say, so this is how we gonna carry it. Fuck Rob, fuck you, and anybody else that called us snitches because we ain't never been no snitches. Now tell us where the fuck is Rob at!"

"Oh you gonna draw on me, little Nigga? You must not know."

The hooded guy waved his hand and the black car from the corner cut on its lights and sped toward them. Dee punched the dude in his face and they ran across the street into an alley. The agents were in a dark blue van on the other side watching

the action unfold. They discreetly followed and were
sure not to blow their cover.

Ricky and Dee ran through the alley
into an East Baltimore slum with the hooded guy and
the black car in hot pursuit. Once in the neighborhood
they ran into a badly charred, abandoned house that
looked like it had been in a very bad fire at some
point. Immediately, the hooded man ran in behind
them and the black car pulled up on the curb. Rob
jumped out of the vehicle with a huge bulge under his
jacket. The agents stayed at the top of the block, just
far enough to observe.

As the agents struggled to get their
equipment straight, they heard shots go off inside the
abandoned house.

Bam! Bam! Bam! Bam! Bam! Bam!

Rob stumbled out of the fire torn
abandoned house holding his bloodied chest and
neck as additional bullets chased him to his car where
he collapsed. There was no sign of the hooded man as

both Ricky and Dee ran out of the abandoned house via the back door. The agents couldn't believe how fast everything happened so they contacted JC and informed of the ordeal. He told them not to blow their cover, so they contacted the local authorities and continued to follow Ricky and Dee.

"Throw the gun, Dee! Get rid of it…" demanded Ricky. He was exhausted from running.

"Fuck that, all we gotta do is catch the bus over to Mondawmin Mall and say we was there the whole time."

"Yo! We might not make it to…"

A police car quickly turned into the alley as Dee tried to toss the gun before running top speed. Ricky tried to run but fell into a very high gate he attempted to scale. One officer threw him to the ground, while the other searched the alley for the gun. Dee was apprehended on the next block, cussing and fussing about his rights.

"This is fucked up! I ain't do nothin! Oww, this shit is hurtin' my wrists!"

****

Meanwhile, agent JC met his agents at a Mc Donald's near Nadet's house. He wanted to brief them on the objectives of the operation. However, he didn't want to tell them exactly what they were looking for. JC knew that if in fact Eboni was still alive, she had to be a very crafty and cunning individual. His agents could serve him best by just following protocol because he wanted all the glory.

"Alright guys, I have Alverez and Lopez watching the boy's house at this moment. We will attain him there. Please don't lose him! Your objective is simple... watch him and report his every move. Do not get involved with his life. Don't interfere with anything he does, whether legal or illegal. I want you to report to me what he does, who he sees, and who he speaks with. That's all I want you to do... any questions?"

"Uh, yes. If you don't want us to interfere with criminal activities, if any, then what are we looking for?"

"Nothing! Again, all I want you to do is stay invisible and report until I tell you it's time to move. Am I clear? If so, then let me hear it!

"Seven!" the agents shouted in unison.

The group of JC's five agents nodded in agreement and went to work. They were hand-picked by JC along with his two best agents, Alverez and Lopez, which made up the magnificent seven. They were the first agents in the FUOCI division of the FBI.

BLACK BUTTERFLY 2 by FEENIX

CHAPTER **VIII**: Almost Midnight?

"Agent JC… come in, come in JC. There is someone approaching the boy's house. We think it's our subject," stated agent Lopez over the radio.

"Good, its eleven twenty-eight pm… record the time and make sure the back door of the house is covered until your relief gets there. JC… out."

From the porch of his grandmother's house, Nadet' could see that every light in the house was on. He looked at his watch, put his key in the front door, and prepared himself for a tongue lashing.

"I know it's not almost midnight and you just walking up in here!" shouted Jackie as Nadet' crossed the threshold.

"Is that him Jackie? Boy, where have you been! We were worried to death about you. I was watching the news…"

"Not now Mama. Nadet', where have you been all this time?" asked Jackie more calmly.

"Aunt Jack... Grandma, I was at Mondawmin Mall with my friends earlier then I caught the wrong bus home and..."

"Mondawmin Mall! That's all the way on the west side! That was unsafe and stupid."

"I know, Aunt Jackie, but we wanted to get these jackets."

"Boy, I don't want to hear about no jackets! Ya'll too old to be dressing alike anyway. That's silly, you know how we worry!"

"I know... I'm sorry Aunt Jackie. I'm sorry Grandma. I guess I didn't think..."

"Go upstairs!" yelled Jackie as she stormed out of the room.

Nadet' put his head down and slowly walked upstairs. His grandmother noticed that his shoes were unusually black and dirty but didn't say anything because the situation was already tense. Jackie never yelled at Nadet' before, so she felt really bad. Halfway up the stairs, Nadet' remembered that he had left his City Paper on the living room table. He came back down the stairs and asked his grandmother if she'd seen it.

"Boy, I ain't seen that curled up thing since your father left... oops."

"My father? What you mean... was he here today, Grandma?"

"Um... it's no use hiding it. Yes, he was here and that's why Jackie is so mad at you. She thought that he may have... well, you know."

"What did he want?"

"He wanted you. I mean... he wants shared custody of you and if he doesn't get it, he's going for full custody."

"What? He can't do that... he's a jailbird! What kind of law is gonna give a child to a known criminal?"

"Anything is possible when you have money and a corrupt system like the one here in Baltimore City."

"Where was he sitting?"

"Well, Jackie was here, I was here, and he wa-s... right there. Right where you are."

"Oh my god! Did he take it?" asked Nadet'.

"I don't know, I can hardly see Day-Day. Ask Jackie, but don't do it now."

"You don't understand Grandma, that paper was very important! It had..."

"I saw you writing in it, why is it so important?"

"Nevermind, I gotta ask Aunt Jackie now!"

******

Meanwhile... Eboni was sleeping in the nanny suite of Patsy's house when she heard the front door open and the alarm go off. She jumped to her feet and slowly crept to her room door. As she peeked through a small crack, she saw Patsy's husband.

"Pat! Where you at? Damn, I told you to pull your car in the garage when you come in for the night!"

Patsy heard her husband's voice and immediately came running. The Wizards weren't scheduled to be home for another week so she wasn't expecting him until then. Eboni put her jogging suit on and climbed out of the window. She heard Zeus fussing and instantly remembered the days when Drake used to fuss and beat her. Eboni often wondered if the same thing was going on with Patsy.

Zeus tried to isolate her; he always wanted her to be alone if he wasn't there.

Patsy didn't tell Zeus that Eboni was staying there because he usually wasn't home due to his NBA schedule. Since the arrangement was supposed to be temporary, Patsy figured it would be easy to conceal. Eboni darted to her car and stayed out of sight.

"Hey Baby, what are you doing home?" asked Patsy.

"What the fuck you mean... what am I doing home? I live here? What... you got a nigga up in here or something?"

"Don't be silly... I'm here like I always am, Baby. I'm just surprised that's all."

"Yeah, leaving both those cars out... when I told you to put them in the fucking garage at night. That's what it's for? I buy the fucking things and you can't even take care of them right."

"Well, I don't see what the problem is. The cars are fine, sometimes I forget…"

"You don't see what the problem is? Are you being a smart ass with me?"

"No, I'm just saying…"

"Naw, you said enough. Maybe you need something to help you with your memory, since you're so forgetful. Come here… now damn it!"

"I didn't mean it like that, I meant…'

As Patsy slowly walked toward Zeus he reached out and snatched her arm. Then he spun Patsy around and to bend her over the couch. Fearfully trying to turn her body, Patsy felt his hands grab her panties and rip them. Zeus pushed Patsy's head forward as he snatched his shorts down to grab his rock hard dick. After spitting on the head of it he commenced to push Patsy's head down to the couch and force himself in her.

"Uh, wait a minute, Zeus. That's hurting me! I'm not wet enough baby... oooow!"

"Naw, you like to get smart and shit. Can't remember, right?"

"You're hurting me..."

Zeus stopped abruptly with a look of disgust on his face. He pulled his shorts up and said, "Get your ass up stairs... I want some pussy. If you can't satisfy me, then I'm gonna have to take matters into my own hands."

"I wasn't complaining, Baby..."

"Look at you... pitiful! Why would anyone wanna fuck that... huh? You better stop gettin' smart with me when I tell you something, girl. Expand your mind... try to see what the fuck I'm saying before you run your mouth."

"Okay Baby," responded Patsy.

"Now, go on upstairs and get that thang ready for daddy. A nigga is stressed out-let's work off some tension."

Zeus continued to fuss as he locked the door and set the alarm. He reeked of liquor and was sweating profusely. Each step he took toward the bedroom sounded like Godzilla crushing Tokyo to Patsy. She nervously stripped naked and waited for Zeus on the bed. The bedroom door knob slowly turned as Zeus rapped numerous obscenities.

"Pussy, pussy, pussy... that's all I need, some good pussy and a bag of weed. Ha, ha, ha! Bitches ain't shit but hoes and tricks. Gum on these nuts and suck the dick."

"Baby, please... that song," whined Patsy.

"That's Snoop Dogg and the Dog Pound's song, baby. I love that shit, plus it's true! Bitches ain't shit! Now turn that ass over."

BLACK BUTTERFLY 2 by FEENIX

DAY Three:

"SECRETS"

FRIDAY

BLACK BUTTERFLY 2 by FEENIX

CHAPTER IX: Investigations

"Agent JC, the local cops are still holding the two boys. Did you want to question them?" asked agent Alverez.

"Question them? Why would I want to do that? All we're supposed to do is follow the Nadet' kid and catch his mom. Stay focused!"

"You don't understand, sir. They're thinking about releasing them this evening."

"What? Two bodies, a motive, and a gun... what do you mean release them?"

"Sir, the gun tossed by the boys wasn't the gun that shot the victims. It was a toy... a pellet gun; they didn't even have any gun powder on their hands. The boys said when they ran into the abandoned house it was dark and they couldn't see. They only heard the shots and assumed that they were coming from the men pursuing them. That's it."

"Bullshit. They're lying!"

"Yea, we know but without a ballistic match or weapon, the alibi might be good enough. The local police went back to the scene to search for the actual weapon involved in the shooting. The only thing we have is the fact they were on the scene with ash on their shoes."

"Ash on their shoes?" asked JC.

"Yeah, the house was in a very bad fire before it was abandoned. I think the boys are guilty but there is nothing that directly connects them at this point. If it was a plan it was a pretty smart one."

"What did you say?"

"I said... if it was a plan it sure was a smart one. Those guys don't seem like..."

"That's it! Oh my god, that's it! Tell the police to hold those boys; I do want to question them."

Agent JC jumped in his car and headed over to central booking with four of his agents following. Once there he went into the prisoner interview room alone and stood in the corner. Both Dee and Rickyy were brought in together.

"Have a seat gentlemen," calmly said JC.

"Who are you?" asked Dee.

"Don't worry about who I am... no wait a minute, maybe you should worry about who I am. Let's just say I'm your worst nightmare, because unlike you, I can do anything I want and get away with it."

Sensing the seriousness of the situation, Rickyy grabbed Dee's arm and pulled him into the chair. Agent JC was a very handsome but intimidating figure; tall, with dark hair, and a very heavy voice. He loved to wear dark suits that were meticulously tailored. Agent JC didn't have time to play and already had a theory of what was going on so he got straight to the point.

"Tell me about Nadet'!"

"Huh? Our friend? What's he got to do with anything?"

"Look, don't play with me because I'll take your little asses to federal prison right now. What happened to Rob and the other guy was planned and both you and I know the two of you aren't the planning types. So, I'm going to say it one more time... tell me about Nadet'."

Rickyy and Dee looked at each other like two deer caught in head lights. They didn't know who this man was exactly, but knew he was someone serious so they didn't want to upset him.

****

Later that day... Drake sat in Mr. Greenberg's office and analyzed the newspaper he stole from Nadet's house. The poem that Eboni had sent Nadet' was highlighted with lots of confused writing around it. When Drake read the poem he immediately knew it was from Eboni, however he too could not make sense of what he was reading.

"Mr. Drake, Mr. Greenberg wants to see you in the upstairs office," said the secretary.

"Aight!"

Drake quickly jogged up the steps and busted into the office, "What you call me for Greenberg? I hope this won't be an everyday thing..."

"Drake... sit down. We have something that needs to be discussed."

"What?"

"John is not doing well. He's taken a turn for the worst."

"What the hell are you talking about Greenberg?"

"John was diagnosed with HIV a few years ago and now it's turned into full blown AIDS. I fear that as his condition worsens he may develop a conscience and pull the plug on everything we've worked for."

"So I won't get my money?"

"No one will. I am going to the hospital this evening to see what state of mind he's in. He's already having second thoughts and like I said, he could blow this whole thing with one word."

"So what do you want from me? I know a set up when I hear one. Be straight up with me."

"Okay then... after I leave, John needs to go! Am I clear? There is a lot of money in it for you."

"Let's do it," replied Drake.

"Good... because after that you need to pay the grandmother another visit."

As Mr. Greenberg and Drake prepared to visit the hospital, John himself made a startling discovery. He found out that Eboni's sister worked at the hospital where he was staying. John's feelings about the whole ordeal began to change after his condition worsened. Plus, he always had his suspicions about Mr. Greenberg and what his true intentions were.

The more he came to terms with the fact that his disease was fatal, the more he wanted to right the wrong he caused. John smiled to himself as he thought of happier times on the set of his show and in life. He remembered how excited Eboni was when she was chosen for the role on his soap opera. How she thanked everyone a million times then let out an exuberant shout halfway down the hallway. He knew she appreciated the opportunity and it felt good to him. Eboni always showed up to the set early, had her lines mastered by show time, and was very easy to work with.

"Hey you... how's it going?" shouted Mr. Greenberg as he entered John's hospital room.

"I'm okay. What brings you here? Is there something we need to go over?" asked John.

"No, I came by to check on you and see how you were feeling. I know that it's been tough for you these last few days."

John wrinkled his face with suspicion. His lawyer was not the type of guy that just "checked on" people, even if they had a life threatening illness. John also noticed that Mr. Greenberg kept suspiciously looking around the room as if he was looking for something. His feelings were confirmed when he got a glimpse of Drake as one of the nurses opened the door to come in.

"Hey Nurse Jackie. I guess it's that time of day again. Thanks for coming by and checking on me Greenberg. The nurse has to take another sample."

"Oh, I can wait. It's no problem John. I'll be over here until she's done."

John knew that there was something going on at that point so he threw out a few test questions. "So how's our boy Drake doing? Is everything going accordingly?"

"Oh, he's fine, everything is looking good."

"Great. When was the last time you spoke to him?"

"John, the nurse is trying to get your blood. We can pick up our conversation in a minute. It's been a few days though."

John's eyes opened wide, he knew that was a lie. He didn't fully know what was going on but, he did know it wasn't good. John quickly decided to fake a seizure in hopes of getting rid of Drake and his lawyer.

"Ugg -Agg –Ah -Um!" John gagged and choked while shaking uncontrollably.

"He's having a seizure," yelled the nurse. She hit the emergency call button next to the bed and ordered Mr. Greenberg out!

As the nurses rushed in to assist, John watched Mr. Greenberg panic and quickly leave. He felt relieved for the moment but his mind kept racing. The situation calmed when it appeared to the nurses that John was coming out of his self-imposed seizure. He looked up and saw nothing but five faces looking back at him. However, one face stood out more than others… it was familiar to him but he didn't know her.

"Nurse Jackie, hold his legs while I get everything else together."

"Okay, Mary. I got him," responded Jackie.

John realized that Jackie was Eboni's sister. He only met her on two occasions when she came to the set and visited Eboni. He remembered her as pleasant and sweet. He tried to make eye contact with her but it was obvious that she wouldn't. Once the head nurse, Mary, was convinced that the situation was under control the others began to leave.

John asked if he could speak with Jackie privately for a minute.

"Yes, how can I help you, Mr. James? It's almost time for my lunch hour," stated Jackie.

"I know that you know who I am because I recognize you and know who you are. Please give a dying man a moment to try and correct a great wrong."

"I'm listening."

"Your sister did nothing wrong. We framed her... and by we, I mean both I and my lawyer. Actually, the part that involved framing your sister was his idea. All I wanted was my ex-wife gone so that she could not destroy my career. My lawyer saw your sister as opportunity. We already know she's not dead but I fear that what I have set in motion is now taking a life of its own... and -it -is - ugly."

"So what do you want from me?" asked Jackie apprehensively.

"Like I said I want to try and right this wrong before I die. I am willing to give a full confession to the police about me and the people involved. I need your help. It will clear your sister's name…"

"Oh my god," Jackie's eyes began to tear. "I'm gonna call our lawyer, he'll know exactly how to handle this. Thank you, Mr. James! I'll be right back."

Jackie darted out of the room to an outside lunch area so she could call Mr. Muhammad. He was thrilled when he heard the news and wanted to hear the confession for himself. Mr. Muhammad asked Jackie to pick him up from his office because he dropped his car to the shop on his way to work. She quickly obliged and hurried to car to get him because she only had an hour for lunch.

John felt good about his decision and closed his eyes to pray for forgiveness. At that moment, his bathroom door slowly opened and Drake silently appeared. He took the opportunity that all the commotion of John's faked seizure caused to hide himself for the right time.

Drake grabbed the extra pillow sitting on a chair in the room and forcefully began to suffocate John. He held the pillow so tight over John's face that lines from the fabric were embedded in his skin when Drake finished. John's severely fragile frame shook for real this time when Drake's massive arms held his head and frame still. Death came silently and violently in a short time for John. Drake immediately slipped out of the room with his hat pulled low over his face.

"Oh my god!" Nurse Mary screamed when she found John lying lifeless in the bed. His nose was broken and blood was streaming down the side of his face. She immediately called security and the doctor on duty.

John was pronounced dead and the doctor on duty could tell it was from suffocation. The police were called in and began to ask everyone who was the last person seen with the victim. Everyone was quiet, no one said a word. They looked at each other and at the ceiling because they loved Jackie.

Reluctantly Nurse Mary said, "Jackie… nurse Jackie Burton was the last one with the victim."

"Has anyone seen her since?" asked one of the officers.

"She ran to the lunch area about forty-five minutes ago," said one of the nurses.

"I want her found. I need to talk to her, now! See if she's still in the building."

CHAPTER X: Nadet's Way

That evening Nadet' left his house with some clothes, sneakers, and other items in a bag from the night before. He caught a bus to the Baltimore Harbor and walked to the subway station. There he caught the first train as it was pulling out of the station down to the next stop and quickly got back on another going in the opposite direction.

"Agent JC... come in," agent Alverez called on his radio.

"This is JC."

"We've lost track of the boy again. He used the subway system to lose us this time."

"Wow, so he must know that we are following him. That's news to me. We have to be pretty damn bad at this when a youngster can out maneuver you. Come on! I thought this was the FBI. What the hell are you doing?"

"Sir, we didn't expect..."

"That's it. We don't know what to expect. Obviously, there's a lot more than meets the eye here. Even his friends won't say a word about him to me. That's a powerful young man and I don't want him taken lightly. Go back to the house and we'll acquire him there. Call me when he gets there. It's time for us to meet face to face!"

Nadet' went to a pet cemetery and buried some bleach soaked clothes and sneakers next to an old tree. He knew that his boys would be okay if they kept their mouths shut. So he decided to swing by their homes to see if they were out yet.

When Nadet' got to Dee's house he saw him surrounded by guys from the block, laughing and joking. He observed for a minute and saw the guys giving Dee money and competing for his attention. They all seemed to be catering to him.

"Yo! What's the deal?" shouted Nadet'.

"Oh, it's my nigga! What's up Baby Boy!" Dee exclaimed. He was over doing it as usual, loud and obnoxious.

"Let me holla at you for a minute, Dee."

Dee pulled away from his new found entourage and went with Nadet, "What's up Day-Day? My main…"

"Nigga, what you doin? Why does it seem like everybody is up your ass? No homo."

Dee laughed, "Yo, word got around that we smoked Rob and his boy. You know how it is in the hood. Niggas are pleading their allegiance. It's happening to Ricky too. I just spoke to him."

"When did ya'll get out?"

"This afternoon. Oh… and there was this one dude there that kept asking us about you but we ain't tell him shit. We thought he was gonna keep us, but he was the main reason they let us go so fast."

"Yo, lose them niggas because all this attention… ain't good."

"Man, are you crazy? We bout to get paid! The word is out… Don't fuck with the Baltimore Boyz! The streets are calling for us! Everybody wants to work for us and with us. Let's get it!"

"Now you trippin'! I'm not fuckin' with it; I still got the situation with my mom to deal with, so if you and Ricky want to play Scarface… go right ahead. Don't call me again when shit gets thick!"

"Yo, wait a minute. I'm not even gonna trip because you did look out for us. You're one of the smartest niggas I know; even the police ain't fuckin with you. Sorry we didn't listen last time when you tried to warn us but if you say leave it alone that's what we gonna do."

Nadet' looked at Dee and said, "I didn't expect to hear that… and definitely not from you."

"You made a believer out of me, Day-Day. Rob never knew what hit him, the cops…

running around like fools, and I'm sitting here with niggas worshipping me because of your ass. Yo, I'm down for whatever!"

"Okay, but right now, I need you to chill. Go to school, get a job, and live normal. My mom would be so disappointed in me if I said anything else."

"The world is yours though… people are waiting on you, Day-Day."

"I don't want the world… I want my mother back. That's all… and I suggest that you go home and hug yours instead of keeping her worried all the time. I mean it Dee, go in the house and hug your mother man. Tell Ricky to do the same. I'll call you later."

Nadet' left Dee a little shaken because the conversation made him remember how much he missed his mother. It was getting dark as Nadet' rode the bus home with thoughts of how his mother became famous ran through his head. The many nights they practiced her scripts, how she use to shout at the world from the kitchen window, and how happy she was when she finally landed the role on *Black Butterfly*.

The back doors of the bus opened and Nadet' got off at his stop. As he walked up the street, the sign that read Cliftview Avenue was illuminated by red, blue and white lights. Nadet' sped up to a slow jog when he realized that there were police lights in front of his house.

"Yo! What's going on? Get out the way. What's wrong?"

As he finally cut through the crowd, he saw the police carrying his aunt Jackie out of the house in hand cuffs. His grandmother was cussing and crying at the front door of the house while several cops blocked her in.

"Get da fuck off my family man!" Nadet' shouted in a violent rage.

"Stand back Son! That's an order. I'm not gonna tell you again," one cop yelled.

Nadet' darted past the first cop, tripped the second cop and grabbed his aunt tight as he could. Agent JC was set up in a house across the street. He had gotten word that the local police were coming for Jackie. JC and his staff continued to observe for fear of blowing their cover as the crowd grew louder. Nadet' wouldn't let go of his aunt as the cops tried to man handle both he and her.

"Leave us alone!" screamed Jackie.

Every time the cops grabbed Nadet', he would bite them, until one grabbed him from behind in a choke hold and slowly peeled him off of his aunt. His feet dangled as he spit, choked, and swung wildly. The crowd grew furious when they saw this and started throwing bottles and rocks at the police cars.

"If them stupid ass cops kill that boy, there's gonna be a riot out here! Let's go," Agent JC ran out of the house with his six agents as the cops called for back-up and started hitting by standers with their Billy clubs.

"Stop! Federal agents. Let us through! Unhand the boy! let him go!" shouted agent JC.

"Take out your badges, maintain order!" said Alverez to the other agents

The crowd separated to let agent JC through but when he pulled out his badge, a cop swung his baton and knocked him to the ground.

"Don't fuckin' move! Stay down," said the cop to JC.

From the ground, JC could see Nadet' still being choked and about to pass out. Before he knew it, JC's temper got the best of him and his fighting skill came in to play. JC snatched the cop's ankle from under him, jumped to his feet as the cop fell, and pulled his nine from the hoister along with his badge. The other agents followed suit as they stood in a circle to hold off everyone.

"Alright, you motherfuckers, this scene is under federal command as of now. A federal agent has been assaulted."

The cops knew they had fucked up. They were frozen with fear... every cop except one, Officer Schwartz, who happened to still be holding Nadet' at the neck. His face completely flustered, Nadet's eyes were starting to roll and there was a bluish color starting to form on his face.

"Asshole! Did you hear me?" JC walked closer to Officer Schwartz, "Let the kid fuckin' go! This scene is under federal command... now!"

The other agents backed JC as the situation between them and the local cops grew more tense. Officer Schwartz smirked before releasing Nadet'. JC had to catch him before his body collapsed to the ground. He looked at Nadet' and was almost brought to tears.

"Alvarez, arrest him!"

"What? You can't do that," Schwartz exclaimed angrily.

"Oh yea? Alvarez, take Officer Schwartz into custody… now!"

The neighborhood cheered as Officer Schwartz was handcuffed and placed in the federal vehicle. JC stood with Nadet' in his arms and motioned for everyone to move out of his way. Immediately, the crowd disbursed to let the ambulance through as the paramedic rushed over to Nadet'. JC didn't want to let him go… not even for the paramedic, somehow he felt connected to the boy. Nadet' opened his eyes as JC laid him on the gurney and said, "Thank You."

The tender moment was interrupted abruptly, "Who's in charge here? You have no right! Release my officer immediately," demanded the police commander just arriving on the scene.

When JC turned to confront the commander he saw the local news crew trying to make it down the narrow street. Smiling in front of a sea of police, JC looked at the commander and said, "Nope."

JC then got into the passenger seat of the federal vehicle with Officer Schwartz handcuffed in the backs and instructed agent Alvarez to slowly pull off. A reporter ran up to the window of the vehicle on JC's side and asked, "Did you really arrest a police officer here tonight?"

"No, I stopped a riot and ensured public safety here tonight... and you can quote me on that!" JC rolled up his window and motioned for Alvarez to move forward. Officer Schwartz yelled statements to the press from a cracked back window.

"He had no right! I was doing my job! You can't arrest a cop!" Officer Schwartz shouted to the reporter.

"Aw, stop cryin'. We're taking you to your captain now, but you will be investigated."

BLACK BUTTERFLY 2 by FEENIX

DAY FOUR:

"EBONI"

SATURDAY

BLACK BUTTERFLY 2 by FEENIX

CHAPTER XI: Unexpected

The next morning Grandma Rose sat in Nadet's hospital room praying heavily because she was so overcome with pain. Her grandson was in the hospital, her daughter in jail, and her vision was fading because of her condition. The only good news was that the doctor said Nadet' was well enough to be released later that evening.

Tap, Tap, Tap!

"Who is it?" Grandma Rose asked as she heard the faint tap.

"It's Fred from Cliftview Ms. Rose!"

"Come on in Fred"

"Are you okay? I wanted to know if you needed anything... if I could help in any way."

Grandma Rose had prayed for some help and felt that God responded that quickly with it.

She looked up to the sky and mouthed "thank you" before answering.

"As a matter of fact, I could use a ride down to the place they took Jackie!"

"Central booking? No problem Ms. Rose, Fortunately, I know exactly where that's at."

Fred and Grandma Rose drove to central booking for a meeting with Mr. Muhammad and Jackie. Fred helped Grandma Rose into the building and waited for her outside the lawyer interview room at central booking.

"Hello, Mr. Muhammad, did you get a chance to find out what's going on?"

"As a matter of fact Ms. Rose, I did find out from an old friend at the police department. A patient at Jackie's hospital was smothered to death and she was the last one seen with him."

"What kinda mess is that? So what she was the last one with him. There's no reason for her to kill nobody!"

"Please calm down Ms. Rose. There's more… and it's not good. Well, the man that was killed was John James."

"The same producer from…"

"Yes, the Eboni ordeal… that's why they think Jackie killed him. To them she had motive. The local media has already linked everything and the blitz is on. It is extremely important that when she comes in you let me speak with her uninterrupted. We have a lot of ground to cover."

****

Meanwhile, back at Nadet's hospital room, he received a note on his lunch tray that read, *Go to the bathroom and put on your clothes. Stay there until someone knocks on the door three times.* Nadet' immediately grabbed his clothes out of the closet and went into the bathroom. A short while later, a nurse knocked three times on the door and walked him to the dock in back of the hospital. Once there, the nurse pointed to a black ford focus with limo tinted windows and said, "Your mother's waiting."

Nadet' slowly walked to the car as the window suddenly rolled down.

"Quickly, Day-Day... get in," said Eboni.

Nadet's eyes widened as he hurried and got into the car. Eboni noticed that the side of his face and neck was bruised and was instantly angered. He hugged and kissed her face repeatedly until her trademark dark shades tilted. Eboni's hands were gloved as she gripped the steering wheel tightly and pulled off.

"Ma, how did you get a car?" asked Nadet'.

"I know people. Sister Diane, the nurse that brought you to me, has been a friend of the family for years. She told me that you were in the hospital and about the Jackie and John situation. This is her car, she's with the movement."

"The movement... what the hell is that?"

"Watch your mouth, that's enough questions. I need you to fill me in Day-Day. Why are you in the hospital? It's all over the news that Jackie was arrested for the murder of John. None of this makes sense."

"Well, I was coming home and I saw the cops bringing Aunt Jackie out so I flipped on them."

"I need to talk to Jackie. Where were you coming from? Nevermind... continue with the story, but we gonna come back to that."

"Like I said, I flipped on them and one cop named Schwartz... I think, grabbed me across my throat and started choking me out. Even when things calmed down I could still feel him applying pressure.

Then this fed dude came out of nowhere and made him stop."

"The feds? They didn't come from nowhere. They must be staked out on the block in one of them houses. It's okay though... the feds keep the local police in check, as you saw. They must be watching you because they know I'm not dead. That's the only thing that makes this a federal case."

"So they've been watching me?"

"I don't know how long, but yes. Do you have anything to hide? Nevermind... can you get in the house from the back?"

"No problem Ma. I got skills."

"Oh yeah, I'm not liking what I'm hearing on the streets about you, Day-Day. We gonna have a talk later about a kid named Black Rob. Okay?"

"Huh? What are you..."

"Before you lie, know that I have eyes everywhere. I told you, I know people. You may never know how far my arm reaches, but know that it does."

Eboni drove the car down the alley behind Cliftview Avenue. It was dark and you could hear the glass breaking under the tires. The dogs were barking so Nadet' quickly got out of the car and ran to the backdoor of the house. Eboni drove the car to Normal Avenue, the next block over and parked. She ran back through the alley, up to the house and in to the basement.

"Ma, am I going with you?"

"No, but I want you to pack a bag for you, your Grandmother, and Jackie... just in case."

"Just in case what" asked Nadet'.

"Just in case of whateva! That's the point; you never know what may happen. Go upstairs and pack the bags then give them to me."

Nadet' ran upstairs to pack the bags while Eboni remained in the basement. As Nadet' passed the front door, on his way up the second flight of stairs, he saw someone watching him through the front window. He played it off like he did not notice and turned to walk back to his mother.

Tap, Tap, Tap!

"Hey Nadet', I know you see me. It's me... your father, let me in. I know she's in there... tell your mother I want to speak to her."

Nadet' darted to the basement-panicked and nervous. Eboni heard the footsteps approaching and quickly pulled her gun.

"Ma, there's a guy outside the window upstairs that says he's my father and he knows you're here," Nadet' whispered.

"Drake is here?"

At that moment, Nadet' and Eboni heard the glass break from an upstairs window. Eboni motioned for Nadet' to stand out of the way and under the steps. She unscrewed the light bulbs to make the basement pitch black before lying on the floor with her gun pointed directly up the stairs.

"Ebon-i... I know you're here Bab-y," sang Drake sarcastically as he stood at the top of the stairs.

"Don't come any closer, it's not gonna be pretty if you do. What do you want?"

Drake heard Nadet's voice but knew it was Eboni's words. She was telling him what to say.

"Oh, so that's how it is now. You can't even talk to me directly... my little brown stallion? It seems like just yesterday when I took that pussy on the carpet at JoJo's house. Even though we were divorced by then, you were still mine... I told you that!"

"Shut up Drake. As usual you're going too far," said Nadet' at Eboni's command.

"No Baby, you went too far when you kept a bastard child without considering my feelings." Drake was trying to frustrate Eboni into speaking directly to him. He wanted to keep her occupied while his two henchmen tried to get in through the basement windows.

Nadet' looked at his mother with a bewildered look on his face as she herself yelled up the stair to Drake.

"You dirty motherfucker! Bring your ass down them steps... I dare you!"

Drake laughed and slowly inched down the steps, "We all know there's only one full blooded killer here. Ask your boy John... oops, you can't... because I took him out. So don't fuck with me little girl. I'm still Daddy to you."

"Biological warfare, motherfucke-r," yelled Eboni as she swung her hand from beneath the steps and stabbed Drake in the leg with something he couldn't identify.

"Oww, shit! It's gonna take more than a prick to stop me, Bitch. Since he couldn't see, Drake kicked in the direction of the attack and caught Eboni in the mouth. She had already fallen to the floor and dropped her gun when Drake's henchmen kicked in the basement windows and started coming in.

Shots rang out from all directions in the darkness of the basement. Drake's henchmen were hit several times as they tried to climb back out the basement windows. Drake himself fired in the darkness without regard for anyone as he retreated back upstairs. His ass burned because he was hit in the lower part of his left cheek by a bullet.

"Yo, get outta there! We'll get her another day," shouted Drake. He ran out the house and back to his car for fear that the police would be called by the neighbors. His boys weren't so lucky, however. They both hung halfway out of the widows, stuck and shaking from numerous gunshot wounds.

"Ma, let's go. The police might be coming." Nadet' grabbed his mother's arm and pulled her toward the steps. She had been grazed by two bullets but was okay. They exited the house by way of the back door, ran down the alley, and went to the car parked on the other street.

"Shit, Day-Day, I left my gun."

"Well, we can't go back now and get it. Was it clean?"

"Yeah, I never touch anything without my gloves on and it was brand new out the box."

Eboni called Diane at the hospital. She wanted to make sure no one noticed Nadet' was gone. Her plan had changed because of Drake; she wanted Nadet' back at the hospital waiting for his grandmother.

"Sister Diane, how's it looking on your end? I need to bring Nadet' back to you and leave the car."

"Everything's cool over here, no one is looking for him. I'll bring his hospital clothes to the dock where you picked him up."

"Great, I'll see you there in ten minutes."

Nadet' didn't want to leave his mother, especially with her bleeding. He felt that he could protect her better than anyone. Eboni didn't even entertain the idea and took notice of the fact that he was changing. Nadet's perspective, his actions, and his thinking were changing because of all he had seen.

"Alright, Day-Day, I need you to go back in there and act like nothing has happened. I know you're good at acting."

"What do you mean by that Ma? Sometimes you gotta do…"

"We don't have time for this conversation right now. Only Diane can reach me so send your messages through her. One more thing…

go get more City Papers and highlight my coded poem to you. Here is the translation, put it in your pocket. Jot it down in the margins; maybe we can use this in reverse. Get Diane's cell number and we'll take it from there."

Eboni reached over and hugged Nadet'. Then she motioned for him to go as she returned Diane's car to the parking garage.

DAY FIVE:

"WEB"

SUNDAY

BLACK BUTTERFLY 2 by FEENIX

CHAPTER XII: Beneath the surface?

Eboni didn't get to Patsy's house until two thirty in the morning. She wasn't sure if Zeus was there or back on the road so she stayed out of sight and crept around to the back of the house. From outside, Eboni could see that Patsy's bathroom light was on and her window open. So she decided to call Patsy from the yard but there was no answer. After calling a few more times, Eboni finally climbed up to the bathroom window from the deck.

Eboni heard some disturbing noises… crashing, loud voices, and what sounded like slapping. She pulled herself up into the window and quietly fell onto the bathroom floor. Once there, the noises became crystal clear.

"Uh, uh, uh… that's it. Fuckin slut."

Slap!

"Give that pussy to daddy. Fuck back bitch… fuck back! Damn, now the wig fell off. Can you do anything right? Move your ass!"

Slap!

"Oww, you're hurting me Zeus. I'm not wet enough. Please, give me a minute. Uh, uh, oww!"

The more Patsy yelled in pain the harder Zeus pounded her. The door was already slightly cracked so Eboni peeked through and saw Patsy wearing a blonde wig, heels, and a belt tied around her neck. She was in doggy position as Zeus's 6'8" frame pounded her 5'2" petite body. He would slap her ass, push her head down, and yank the belt back up at will. It was dark but she looked to be in excruciating pain.

"Uh, Uh, Uh, Yeah, Bitch! I'm gettin this motherfucker! Yeah…"

"Owww, stop! Stop it! You're choking me!"

"Get the fuck up then," Zeus slapped Patsy off the bed and hurled insults at her. "Damn, you fuck up anything. A nigga can't even get his nut off wit you complaining and shit. You need to be a real woman and please your man. That's exactly why niggas go out here and do what we do!"

Patsy lied on the floor for a minute to get herself together. Her insides were on fire. She clutched her stomach as she got up and slowly walked to the bathroom before she urinated on herself.

"Baby, sometimes you're too rough. I can't do it no more tonight."

"Man, come on. Don't gimmie that. I still haven't even came yet… shit! When you finish in the bathroom, see if you can at least suck this dick right. You can't leave your man unsatisfied like that."

"Okay baby, uh, just let me go to the bathroom."

Patsy walked into the bathroom and shut the door behind her. Eboni was standing in the shower looking at her with tears in her eyes. Patsy's whole body was red with hand prints all over. Her neck was badly bruised and she had a little piece of dried up blood on the side of her mouth.

Eboni whispered, "Tell me... does he do this all the time?"

"He just likes rough sex... it's okay."

Eboni turned on the sink and shower water full blast to drown out any sound in the bathroom. She took off her jeans, rolled up her sleeves, and grabbed the robe from the door. "Gimmie that fuckin' wig."

Eboni snatched the wig off of Patsy's head then went into the cabinets and pulled out some super hold hairspray, super glue, KY Jelly, and a plunger. As she unscrewed the plunger from its base, Patsy's lip quivered and she kept shaking her head no to Eboni.

140

"Please, don't Eboni... Please."

"You can't help him now. Listen to me, Pat... you got two choices; one, I call the cops and let them see your face and body all beaten...he will be on the news by morning and his career will be over. Or two, you put on my clothes and climb your ass out that window and help him when I'm finished. You got two seconds to decide."

"Damn, what the fuck is taking so long! Take your shower later, my shit is going down," yelled Zeus as he lay on the bed with one hand behind his head and the other stroking his dick.

Then the bathroom light went out and the door opened. A shadowy figure, hunched over, limped toward Zeus.

"It's about time. Why you cut out the bathroom light though? I can't see shit now."

The shadowy figure grabbed his dick and stroked gently-simultaneously squirting KY Jelly between his dick, balls, and ass. The figure had Zeus's full cooperation.

"Aw shit, that's what I'm talking about, Baby. Bring it back for daddy!"

The figure breathed on the head and down the shaft as she moved more of the jelly to his ass with her fingers. She stroked his dick harder and faster taking small licks periodically.

"Oh yeah, oh yeah, suck it. Suck it, Bitch, suck it!" Zeus grabbed a hand full of her hair in the wig and pushed her head to his dick as he pumped. All of a sudden a loud sound from something breaking came out of the bathroom.

"What the fuck is that?" he yelled at the door as the bathroom light came on and Patsy ran out.

"What the fuck... owwwwwwwwwwwww!"

Zeus let out a piercing high pitched scream as Eboni clamped down on his dick with her teeth and simultaneously shoved the plunger handle up his ass. He flung her by her hair off the side of the bed as she reached into the robe pocket and sprayed him in the eyes with the holding spray.

Zeus fell off the bed holding his private and rubbing his eyes. Eboni stood up, pushed Patsy away, and squeezed an entire tube of crazy glue over his hand and private area.

"Now explain to the cops why your hands are glued to your dick and your plunger handle got shit on it. Now touch her again and I promise you..."

"Fuck you, Bitch! Awwwww, fuck you!"

"Fuck me? Fuck me, huh?"

Eboni darted to the bathroom to grab some rubbing alcohol and a lighter out of her jeans. When she came back in the room, Zeus was bleeding and standing up. He was screaming in pain because one of his hands was still stuck to his groin.

"Fuck me, huh?"

Woosh! Woosh!

Eboni threw the whole bottle of rubbing alcohol on Zeus. He tried to charge her but was in to much pain to catch her as she retreated back into the bathroom and grabbed his can of spray deodorant. Eboni lit the lighter and held the deodorant directly behind the flame.

"Alright, Bitch! I'm going to ask one more time. Are you going to put your hands on her again?"

"Stop, Eboni, please!" begged Patsy.

"I don't mean no harm Pat, but if this motherfucker don't answer me real soon..."

Eboni pressed the aerosol and made the flame ignite like a torch close to Zeus. Both he and Patsy jumped back.

"I'm gonna fry the shit out of him like some pork skins! I'm sorry girl."

"Aight, I won't touch her! I need a doctor man. I'm fuckin' losin' all types of blood over here!"

Eboni quickly took off her robe and grabbed her jeans before she bolted down the steps then out the front door. She was losing it; her situation was growing worse by the minute. There was no safe place for her to turn except one... God. But how could she turn to him after all that she had willingly done, with all the hate she had bottled up inside? Sure she had been falsely accused of Madeline's death but since that time, she had really become a killer in her own right. Eboni was confused but took the first step and made the call she never wanted to make.

BLACK BUTTERFLY 2 by FEENIX

CHAPTER XIII: What's Really Going On?

Later that morning the doctor released Nadet' from the hospital to his grandmother and they were met by the police. Nadet's grandmother was dropped off by Fred after their meetings so she never went back home. She expected the doctor to release Nadet' the day before so to her, there was no need at the time. After Nadet' got back to the hospital, he told his doctor that he'd felt like he needed one more day, so the doctor granted it to him.

"Ms. Burton, we need you and the boy to come with us for your own safety." The detective was very careful with them in light of the pending case with Jackie.

"Where are we going officer?" asked Nadet'.

"We are going to the station to talk. There's some really important things we need to discuss."

Nadet' and his grandmother rode down to the station and sat in the interview room. Agent JC and two from his team were already on the other side of the double sided glass, brainstorming.

"Okay, this is getting ridiculous. There's a lot going on here but most of all, there's a lot of mistakes," said agent JC.

"Okay, so Alvarez... you verified that the boy never left the hospital last night, right?"

Alvarez nodded yes then looked away because he didn't stay at the hospital where Nadet' was. He decided to follow the grandmother and Fred all day.

"Okay. Two dead bodies with no ID and a syringe, right?" JC asked Lopez as he nodded yes.

"I can't believe that out of seven agents, no one thought to cover the house last night. At least we have the murder weapon on the scene, right Detective?"

148

"Well, we have a weapon but it's not the murder weapon. It hasn't even be fired," said Detective Ross, the lead detective on Jackie's case.

"Not again! This is bullshit; someone is making us look like fools!"

"That's because we were not working together with the local police initially. Now that we are…" said agent Lopez.

"We were not working with them because we have two different agendas. I don't want to lose focus and that's what we seem to be doing. We are here to find the girl! Not solve homicides, chase drug dealers, or stop riots. We have not found the girl because we are getting caught up in all this drama. However, I do have theory and the shit is about to hit the fan."

"So, what's the theory JC?" asked Alvarez.

"You guys are not ready for this one. Trust me; they gonna be talking about this one for a long time if I'm right."

"I know what I want to do... Detective Ross! Do a rush on the ballistics for the bullets that were in the two men at the house. I need it like yesterday! Alvarez... get me the ballistics from the drug dealers killed in the abandon house a few days ago."

"Agent JC, what about the boy and his grandmother? Should we let them go," asked Detective Ross.

"Yes, and see if you can arrange for the sister to be released."

"What? That's an open and shut case. We have motive and opportunity."

"You have nothing because she didn't do it. I don't know who did but she didn't; besides even the motive is not air tight. There are at least a dozen witnesses that say he asked to see her, she doesn't have any priors, and there is no physical evidence. You don't have hair, skin, or clothing fibers from her. Even the public Defender's office can win that case. Let her go!"

"Okay, you have a point but now we're back to square one."

"Exactly, whoever did kill John likes the fact that Jackie took the fall. When she's out, they may show their ugly little head. Make it happen!"

BLACK BUTTERFLY 2 by FEENIX

CHAPTER **XIV**: "Plans"

"Damn Greenberg, I had her! She was right there..." spewed Drake.

"And she shot you in the ass. Would you give it a rest already? It's been almost two days. You're lucky that it was only a flesh wound. Marco and Jason weren't so lucky."

"That's okay though, I'm going to get her ass. I figured out her little coded poem in the paper."

"How do you know it's from her?"

"Well, for one thing the boy had it circled. Plus I know her writing; it's something we both could do. A writing style is like a fingerprint... unique to that person. Now I know where she's gonna be and when."

"Really, I've got to hear this genius...," sarcastically remarked Mr. Greenberg.

BLACK BUTTERFLY 2 by FEENIX

"Okay, read this…" said Drake.

I call you sun because you shine like one. In the garden, one sees the sun many times. But in seven days I plan to sea the sunrise. All because natural things have family ties… like the sun, mother earth, and sibling butterflies. Why oh why did the butterfly convert time to 180 degrees of nine?

"Lovely…" remarked Mr. Greenberg.

"Now, the boy had already done some in the margin, so all I had to do was finish it. Check it out."

Translation: She's proud of him. Every week she sees him in sound garden getting the paper. In seven days meet her at the harbor. She wants it to be Nadet', her mother, and Jackie… At 6:00.

"There ya go!"

"That's pretty impressive Drake, but seven days from when?"

"I'm assuming that since the City Paper comes out on Wednesday, she means seven days from that!"

****

Later that evening... The police released Jackie from custody at agent JC's suggestion. Grandma, Nadet', and Mr. Muhammad stayed at the station and waited for her. Overjoyed, they left the station and headed back to Cliftview Avenue. Nadet' remembered that his mother asked him to get more City Papers, so he asked them to stop.

Once they arrived back home, they saw a house that still looked like a crime scene. Mr. Muhammad called the lead detective in to see if he could shed some light on the situation.

"Detective Ross, have you guys figured anything out? Is the family safe here?" asked Mr. Muhammad.

"Well, it's too early in the investigation for us to make any judgment calls. If they feel unsafe, they should stay somewhere else."

"Do we have a motive, an ID on the two victims, anything?"

"No. Like I said, it's too early in the investigation. Even after we find out who the victims are, what were they doing there? The family said they never saw them before when we showed them the pictures. We need to know who shot them and why was that person in the house? We just don't know anything."

"Okay detective. If you need them again, you know where to find me."

Click!

"Okay Grandma Rose, the detectives don't have any answers, but did say maybe you should stay somewhere else if you don't feel safe."

"I'm not letting anybody run me away from my own home! We are fine. Jackie, call somebody to fix those basement windows and put some bars on them."

"Okay Mama," replied Jackie.

"Nadet', call them two hoodlum friends of yours over here to help clean up."

"Okay Grandma," Nadet' answered.

"Looks like you got it all under control Ms. Rose. I'll call you if anything new develops," said Mr. Muhammad."

BLACK BUTTERFLY 2 by FEENIX

CHAPTER XV: Ducks In A Row

After cleaning up that night, Nadet' sat down to speak with Ricky and Dee at the house. He told them that he was gonna need their help with some very important things. They, of course, were down for whatever he wanted to do. Nadet' decided to call Sister Diane so she could contact his mother for further instructions.

Sister Diane informed Nadet' that his mother wanted him to highlight and translate the poem in the margins of the newspaper. She also wanted him to make sure all interested parties somehow gained access to it. He didn't understand but planned to do what his mother asked.

"Yo Day-Day, me and Rickyy like the name Baltimore Boyz, that's what they keep callin us anyway," said Dee.

"What's the Baltimore Boyz?"

"That's us… the name of our click! My name is Gunz and Rickyy name is Wisdom… call him Wiz for short. So now, you gotta get a street legal name!"

"Huh? Man, I told you… I ain't with that shit. I did what I did to help ya'll out of a jam, that's it. I'm focusing on other shit right now and I need ya'll help, okay?"

"Okay man, no problem. You know we got your back brother."

"Oh, by the way, has anybody seen that snitch ass nigga Chucky around?"

"Naw, that dude is ghost like a mutha! He must have heard what the Baltimore Boyz did to Rob and got the fuck outta dodge," laughed Dee. Both he and Rickyy had a look of hunger in their eyes Nadet' had never seen before. It was destructive and self-serving yet simple and not hard to understand at all. That look scared him because he knew it was a bottomless pit.

"That's good he left."

"Yo Day-Day, I heard some cop choked you out for no reason at all. Is that true," asked Ricky.

"Yeah, that's how they are around here. But I'll see that fat motherfucker again in this life or the next."

BLACK BUTTERFLY 2 by FEENIX

DAY SIX:

"Countdown"

MONDAY

BLACK BUTTERFLY 2 by FEENIX

CHAPTER XVI: "Connect The Dots"

Monday Morning ...

"Oh my God, JC! You are a genius! How did you know? What does all this mean," asked Agent Alvarez.

JC smirked then shook his head before saying, "I was kinda hoping I was wrong this time, but I can tell by your reaction that I wasn't. Let me guess you have ballistics from both crime scenes, right?"

"Yep," said Alvarez

"They match perfectly, huh?"

"Yep, and it's freaking me out because I don't know what that means but I'm sure you do, JC."

"Yep," responded JC.

"So you're not gonna tell us how the same phantom gun in the Black Rob murder showed up at the Cliftveiw Avenue murders?"

"I can't right now. I have my theories, but that's all they are. We are much closer now. Get the agents together; we are going to pay that house a visit."

JC and his agent drove to the stakeout house on Cliftveiw. He instructed Lopez and Alvarez to go inside and question the family while they plant a wire and look for clues.

"Plant a wire? Aww man JC! We need a court order for that."

"We are the federal government; we don't need anything but opportunity. Just do what I say and let me worry about the paperwork."

"You're the boss…"

The agents went over to Nadet's house and knocked on the door. Everyone was in the kitchen eating before Jackie opened the door.

"Federal Agents… may we come in for a minute? We'd like to ask you a few questions," said Lopez as he flashed his badge.

"Call the lawyer," yelled Grandma.

Nadet' grabbed one of the City Papers and walked to the living room. He sat down on the couch and laid the paper on the coffee table with the poem exposed.

"Nadet', excuse us," said Jackie.

"Oh… okay Aunt Jackie, my fault." Nadet' quickly darted up the stairs but listened at the top.

The agents sat in the living room on the couch where Nadet' previously sat. Lopez noticed the news paper immediately and commented. He picked it up and started thumbing through.

"Wow, I was looking for a paper. I wanted to check out some of this Baltimore real estate."

"I don't think that's what you guys came here to talk about," said Grandma Rose as she sat in the arm chair across from the agents.

"You're right, Ms. Rose. We didn't come here to talk about real estate, but we also didn't come here to interrogate your family either. Call your lawyer if you like, but we just wanna talk."

"Forgive us, but we've not had good experiences with the police," said Jackie.

"I understand, but we are not the police. We actually checked the police the last time as I recalled… and we are the reason you, Jackie, are free now."

Jackie paused and thought for a second then said, "You're right. What would you like to talk about?"

"Thank you, but can I trouble you for a cup of water? I'm dying of thirst."

"No problem Mr. Lopez, I'll be right back," said Jackie.

As Jackie went into the kitchen agent Alvarez distracted Grandma Rose with the newspaper as Lopez planted two bugs in the living room. One bug was placed under the coffee table and the other was along the top of the lamp shade.

"Here's your water Mr. Lopez."

"Thank you. I want you to tell me exactly what John said to you when you spoke in the hospital."

BLACK BUTTERFLY 2 by FEENIX

CHAPTER **XVII**: "Ouch!"

"Hello Mr. Drake, we ordered lunch a few minutes ago… want me to get you something?" asked the secretary at Mr. Greenberg's office.

"I'm okay. Is Greenberg in the back?"

"Yes, you can go back. He's waiting for you. Sure you wouldn't like anything?"

"I'm sure Baby. My leg is fuckin' hurtin' like a big dog! I don't know what's wrong with me," said Drake as he walked into Mr. Greenberg's office.

"Drake! How's my main homie?" laughed Mr. Greenberg as Drake entered the room.

"Don't ever use that word again. You wouldn't know what a homie was if one kicked you in the face. Man, I need to see a doctor. I ain't playin no more. I have a lump on my leg with puss in it."

"Okay, okay Drake. Hey Alice, call Doctor Forman and tell him to get his ass over here ASAP. It's an emergency," Mr. Greenberg told his secretary on the intercom.

"Yes Sir, Mr. Greenberg," said the secretary.

"You happy now Drake? The doc is on his way, cry baby."

"Man, I'm serious. Please take a look at this thing for me."

Drake lifted his pants leg and exposed a big purple puss filled lump. He got a tissue from the desk and busted the bump as he yelled. Mr. Greenberg wrinkled his face disgusted by the sight. When Drake moved the tissue from the bump they saw a speck just beyond the surface. Mr. Greenberg grabbed some tweezers from his desk drawer and picked at the speck.

"Ow... owwww... shit, that hurts Greenberg," yelled Drake.

"Quiet, I almost got it Drake. What -the fuck -is –this? Look Drake…" demanded Mr. Greenberg as he pulled a long thin pin like metal out of the sore.

"Damn, it looks like a long ass needle or something?"

"That's exactly what it is…"

"Yo, that's what she stabbed me with. When I came down the steps…"

"The girl? Why didn't she use a knife? That doesn't make sense unless that's the closest thing she had."

Both men looked up and the doctor was standing in the door way. He walked toward them with a concerned look on his face and a cellophane bag in his hand.

"Give me that, it needs to be tested. I assume this is why you called me over. Let me take a look at that son."

"Okay Doc. It's been hurting a few days now. Maybe I need to come in and be checked out."

"I agree; this-at the very least-is infected. We need to get you there right now."

"Why? What's that look on your face about doc? That shit scares me."

"I'm always concerned when I see a needle that it's a bio-hazardous. I want to run some test on you and the needle as a precaution."

"Go with the doctor Drake. We can handle our business later," said Mr. Greenberg.

Drake followed the doctor to the hospital and kept his cool. He hated seeing doctors like most men, but complied anyway. All he could think about was the payback on his ride over there.

CHAPTER **XVIII**: "Naked Lil Niggas"

Later that night... Nadet' was speaking to Ricky and Dee in his back yard.

"The Feds stopped by here today."

"Oh Shit! What they want?" asked Dee.

Ricky and Dee stood there in suspense with their mouths open and rubbing their head.

"They're still tryin' to catch my mother. They want to see if she's gonna contact me."

"Your mother? No disrespect Son-Son, but didn't your mom's pass?"

"Naw, I just saw her and that's all I'm gonna say right now."

"Oh shit! I thought you were just trying to work on some stuff for the insurance jump off. I had no idea she was still..."

"Don't repeat that, but I told you shit was thick. As a matter of fact, Sister Diane is her friend."

"Yo Nadet', guess what?" said Ricky.

"What?"

"That dude Chucky done popped up. He's talkin' a lot of smack too. Sayin he ain't hiding, we the snitches, and that our day is comin'."

"Oh, yeah?"

"Yeah, he said that Baltimore Boyz' shit ain't real. We ain't keeping it one hundred. I wanna smash that nigga with the quickness," replied Ricky.

"Focus Man! He's just a distraction right now. His day is comin, trust me. I let you know, but for right now... keep a cool head, mon." They all giggled when Nadet' did his Jamaican accent from Shottas which was their favorite movie.

"So, why did you call us here tonight?"

"I need ya'll to help me with something. I don't need you to do much, but I need you to be on point."

"Alright, but why is everything so covert with you? Why we gotta figure shit out all the time."

"I'll explain on the way to our destination. Here… take this digital camera, voice recorder, and Aunt Jackie's hooded shawl."

"Yo, you mad crazy dog. Why in the hell do you have on gloves when it's not even cold out here?" Dee jokingly said.

Nadet' explained half of his plan to his friends to calm their nerves as they all walked down to Clifton Park. He kept the other half to himself which was normal for him. On the way, he placed a call to Drake. Nadet' saved the number from the card he left at the house.

"Hello… d-d-dad?"

"Dad? Oh damn, is that you Day-Day?"

"Yeah, I just wanted to thank you."

"Huh? For what, lil man?"

"For killin' Mr. John," Nadet' pretended to sniffle then continued, "he ruined our lives. Mom just doesn't understand how much I hated him."

Drake was surprised to hear from Nadet' but what he said made sense. He immediately wanted to take advantage of that emotional situation.

"Well... I always loved your mom and I would never let anybody get away with hurting her. Have you seen her today?"

"Nah, I'm supposed to meet her here in a few minutes though."

"Where is here?"

"At Clifton Park, near the pool area. She should be on her way."

"Okay. Well like I said... I still love her. Can you put in a good word for me? Don't tell her you talked to me though, okay? Ya'll be safe tonight."

Drake hung up the phone and sped to the location like Nadet' knew he would. Everybody got into their position... Dee put on the shawl with the voice recorder in his pocket and Ricky hid on top of the pool house with the digital video camera. Nadet' sat at the focal point under a tree and waited with his jacket on. After a moment Ricky shouted to Nadet'.

"Yo, get ready! I see a car pulling up with their lights off."

"Look through the camera and zoom in. See if it's a medium built man, with curly black hair, and acting suspicious."

"Well... he's got on a hat, but he's definitely acting suspicious."

"Cool. Once he spots me, signal Dee to walk over to me with the shawl."

Drake tip toed to a tree and looked around before spotting Nadet'. He then eased his way to a better position as Dee walked up with the shawl on. Dee hugged Nadet' like he was Eboni and then pretended to talk as Dee kept the shawl hood on. Drake observed and was convinced it was Eboni so he walked up on them with his gun out.

"So we meet again my sweet, sweet princess. Don't you love family reunions?"

Dee turned around and put his hands up, while Nadet' pulled his black nine millimeter from his jacket. Drake's eyes widened when he saw the gun and the fact that Dee was not Eboni.

"Where the fuck is your mother? I can't believe it... are you fuckin' with me?"

Nadet' didn't answer; he pretended to be nervous by making his hand shake. However, Dee was very nervous because he did not know that guns were going to be involved. Drake was furious and got more aggressive.

"Look, lil nigga, I will merc your ass right now and think of it as a really late abortion. Give me the gun now!"

Nadet' pretended to cry and said, "Don't hurt us... I just want you to leave my mother alone."

"I won't hurt you if you give me the gun! Now give it to me."

Drake walked over to Nadet' and slowly grabbed the gun as he lowered it. Dee was looking at Nadet' like he was out of his mind.

"Why you gonna give him the gun? He gonna kill our ass," whispered Dee.

After getting the gun from Nadet', Drake laughed and shook his head. He looked at the gun and noticed that it didn't have bullets and began to laugh.

"This is a good ass gun, it's better than mine. But if you ever draw on somebody again, make

sure you got bullets. This street thang ain't for you.
Ya'll little niggas gonna get yourselves killed out this
motherfucker."

"Please don't hurt us," begged Nadet'.

"I ain't gonna do nothin to ya'll but I
want you to give your mother this message, meet me
at Sound Garden at 6:00 pm alone. I know that she
already planned on being there, if she doesn't show
up, you and your mother will pay dearly for her
mistake. Now strip lil niggas!"

"Huh," Nadet' and Dee said in unison.

"I said take off all your shit and I mean
everything. Ya'll little bitches embarrassed me by
having me out here like a fool, so now it's your turn.
Strip niggas!"

"Aww man, this is fucked up. You
serious?"

Drake pointed his gun and cocked it.
I'm gonna start knee capping in ten seconds if I don't

see clothes coming off. I killed John's gay ass, no pun intended. Don't think I won't! One... two... three..."

"Alright, alright... keep a cool head."

Nadet' and Dee stripped down to nothing. They covered their crotch with their hands and laid the clothes on the ground in a pile. Drake laughed and picked the clothes up.

"Now that's gangsta, lil niggas! The next time you decided to play with me... don't. I'm not usually this nice. Deliver the message!"

Drake jogged off toward his car as Nadet' and Dee ran to a dark corner. Ricky came down from off the roof laughing.

"Yo, I got all dat! You was scared as shit Day-Day. Why did you let him take your gun?"

"Because I wanted him to," replied Nadet' as he took Ricky's cell phone and called the police to pick them up.

BLACK BUTTERFLY 2 by FEENIX

DAY SEVEN:

"MACHIAVELLI"

TUESDAY

BLACK BUTTERFLY 2 by FEENIX

CHAPTER **XIX**: "Rendezvous"

The next morning Nadet' deleted the camera footage down to where Drake had the gun on them and made them strip. He did the same with the voice recorder and deleted it down to the confession. Nadet' and Dee were scheduled to talk to the police today because they acted so traumatized the night before when they were picked up naked. Detective Ross and JC's two agents came to Nadet' grandmother's house to get the statements.

"I called Drake from my cell. I got the number from the card he left Aunt Jackie when he was here. I just wanted to see him. He's the only parent I got left," said Nadet'.

"So what did he say to you on the phone?"

"He started talking about how much he loved my mother and how he wanted to protect me. He saw the whole thing on TV when I was in jail and it made him really angry. I was crying a little so he told me to meet him at the park. He said don't worry because he had everything under control."

"You said that you had recordings of him," asked Lopez.

"Yeah, here they go right here. I knew how Aunt Jackie and Grandma felt about Drake so I couldn't tell them where I was going. I was really nervous so I called Dee and Ricky to go with me. We always tape ourselves rapping, cracking jokes, or just kickin' it so I thought that this was definitely worth taping. Plus, I didn't trust Drake."

"Didn't trust him? But you called him, according to your own statement."

"Yeah I know, but as the time got closer and closer, I grew more nervous about the meeting."

"Okay, so what did he do next?"

"He rolled up on us near the pool talking all nice then flipped when I couldn't tell him anything about my mother."

"Your mother? What would she have to do with this?"

"I don't know because she's been dead for months. I really didn't understand his questions and that frustrated him. He pulled out a gun then told us to take off our clothes or he would kill us because we embarrassed him."

"Don't worry, we'll get him. Detective Ross put an APB out on this asshole. Is there anything else we should know?"

"Oh yeah, he said that it was him that killed Mr. John at Aunt Jackie's job."

"What? Are you sure that's what you heard? I need you to be one hundred percent sure," said Lopez.

"Me and Dee heard it. It's even on the recorder I think."

"You said he pointed a gun at you and your friend, right?"

"Yeah, that dude had a nine pointed right in my face. I'll never forget that."

"A nine millimeter automatic handgun?"

"That's what it looked like to me. I damn sure wasn't asking any questions… oops, sorry Grandma."

"Okay, we need to pick him up now. That gun might be the missing link we need!"

Detective Ross from the Baltimore Police Department put out an APB on Drake, while Lopez shared the intel with JC.

"Let me get this right: the kid said that his dad was asking about his mom, got angry, pulled a gun and made him strip? That only makes sense if the dad knew what we know… the mother is still alive," stated JC.

BLACK BUTTERFLY 2 by FEENIX

"What we don't know, is why he's looking for her and why he killed John," replied Alvarez.

"Hold on a minute, we're still not positive the kid's father killed John. All we have is the kid's word and this taped conversation. We need to see if he has the murder weapon."

"If he does, it blows all old scenarios out the water and this really doesn't make sense," said Lopez.

"Oh it makes sense alright... that's the problem. It's so-o-o neat."

BLACK BUTTERFLY 2 by FEENIX

CHAPTER XX: "Drake 2"

That afternoon Drake got a message from the doctor's office about the results of the tests. They wanted him to call back soon as possible.

"Hello, my name is Drake... patient number #20006. I'm supposed to ask for Dr. Yamchick."

"Okay, I have you right here, I'm going to put you through, hold please."

"Hello, this is Dr. Yamchick."

"Hey Doc, this is Drake. Your office called me earlier today."

"Yeah Drake, um, I need to talk to you about the test we ran on you and the needle tip we pulled from your leg."

"Okay, spit it out doc."

"Well, the sore itself was nothing but an irritation and infection caused by the needle tip being beneath the skin. Once removed and with the proper antibiotics the pain should stop then go away."

"Yeah, it feels better already. Even the swelling is gone."

"Good, but the problem is the needle tip. We fear that you may have been injected with something prior to the tip breaking from the syringe. We flushed the needle point and it appears to have another blood type in it. This leads us to believe that you may have been injected with someone or some thing's blood."

"What? Why would someone do that and how can that affect me? I feel great, except for a slight cold."

"Well Drake, we attempted to test the small amount of blood from the needle tip and it appears to be HIV positive. We're not sure though because we didn't have enough of it to conclusively..."

"Get the fuck outta here! HIV? Are you telling me I was injected with AIDS?"

"I'm not saying that, we simply don't have enough information. It's only a possibility at this point. We need you to come in so we can run some more tests. Calm down."

"Don't tell me to calm down. The chances are greater than you think that I may have something because of who stabbed me with the needle. That bitch is gonna die! I will be in tomorrow for the test but I got something to do right now. Goodbye, Doc."

Drake grabbed his gun and packed a bag for himself. He knew Eboni was supposed to be at Sound Garden by six and he was going to be prepared. Drake took the gun he got from Nadet' and began to load it as well. Then his cell phone rang with a call from Mr. Greenberg.

"Drake! Where are you?"

"I'm at the crib, why?'

"I just been notified as your lawyer that the cops have a warrant for your arrest and they are headed to you apartment right now. Get the fuck out of there!"

"What! Oh, that's some bullshit. I ain't going back to jail!"

Drake looked out his eighth floor window and saw the cars coming down the block with their lights on but no sirens. He grabbed his bag and headed out onto the fire escape at the back of the apartment building. He was in such a hurry that he left the other gun he was loading on the kitchen table.

"Alvarez and Lopez, go around the back," ordered JC. "Johnson and Williams, come with me and the detective into the building.

Detective Ross ordered his officers to surround the building and to get tactically ready for anything as they went in. The cops slowly crept up the stairs, checking every open space. They told everyone to lock their doors and to get out of the hallway. When they got to Drake's unit, they listened first at the door then yelled police and kicked it in.

Boom!

"Police, Police, if anyone is in here, come out now with your hands up!"

Once the area was secured, they walked through and noticed that they must have barely missed him. The bathroom sink was running, the closet and drawers were ram-sacked and most of all there was a partially loaded nine millimeter hand gun on the kitchen table.

"JC, we have a weapon right here!" yelled Lopez.

"Great! Your only mission in life Lopez, is to test this gun and see if it matches the bullets from the other two crime scenes. Go, go, go!" JC shouted at the top of his lungs. "Detective Ross! Make sure your people tear this place apart looking for clues and let me know when you catch him. Me and my agents have an appointment with a ghost at Sound Garden. Move out!"

JC and his people got in their vehicles and headed to Fells Point. Two of his other agents were watching the house and were waiting to follow Nadet' to the location.

Nadet' spoke with Sister Diane on the phone in code and she told him that his mother wanted him to go to Sound Garden and just look at records for about an hour. Eboni herself had a small team of supporters with her and they were just going to hang back and watch how many agents, police, enemies, press, etc. would show up. She wanted to know how many people were really on to her.

Nadet' met up with his friends, put on his Ipod, and headed down to the store. The agents followed the bus he was on and stayed in contact with JC on the radio to alert him of Nadet's moves. The boys were laughing and joking the whole way down to Sound Garden. Nadet' was having lots of fun because he knew that he was leading the police on a wild goose chase along with his mother. It brought him a certain satisfaction and sense of power to do that. He hated cops because he saw so much police corruption in his short life.

Once at Sound Garden, the boys went inside, listened to CD's, looked at DVD cases, and flirted with the girls working there. Basically, they were killing time. JC and his agents covered all angles of the building and grew tired of waiting outside.

"Johnson and Williams, he's never seen you... go inside and act like customers just in case she's already inside."

Johnson and Williams went in one at a time and pretended to look around the store. Nadet' knew they were agents right away because they looked so out of place.

He kept picking up police DVD's and talking loudly about how stupid the cops were in the movies.

Eboni had had two people from her movement working in the store. They kept her up-to-date on the action via their earpieces and cell phones. She and a few of her people were staked out at the Kalis Court restaurant across the parking lot. After about an hour, Jones and Alvarez came into the restaurant and got a table right beside hers to watch the very same store. They were talking to each other and Eboni was getting all the info she needed.

"Man, is JC sure she's not dead? I haven't seen a thing since we began this investigation," said Alvarez.

"I don't know, maybe she got here before us and saw us pull up. Either way, this is a waste of time right here. No one is gonna show up. We're not living up to our magnificent seven moniker. JC is gonna have to take his loss on this one."

Eboni wrote down everything she heard them talking about while Nadet' was in the store wondering why Drake hadn't showed up. This was the perfect time for the cops to catch him. Two hours went by, and as the agents grew tired and frustrated, the boys finally decided to leave.

"Oh well, back to the drawing board!" JC exclaimed. His cell phone rang and it was Lopez with the ballistic results.

"Hey JC, I got the results back and the gun is a perfect match. This is the weapon used in both crimes. Unfortunately, I spoke with the local police and it appears that Drake is gone. No trace of him, even his lawyer cannot get in contact with him. He's scared; he thinks the guy may have gone over the edge also."

"That's funny. He helps people get away with murder all the time and now he's scared. The irony is amazing. I tell ya what, you go and stay with him tonight, just in case. Let Alverez watch the kid tonight by himself. The rest of us will check the trains, planes, and automobiles headed out of town to see what we come up with. We all will re-group tomorrow morning at 8:00 am sharp!"

"Okay, boss, don't worry. We'll get him and the boy's mother."

"I know we will. You and Alvarez get some rest tonight. It should be quiet."

CHAPTER **XXI**: "Got My Back?"

As Nadet' and his friends rode the bus home from Sound Garden, they kept talking about being the Baltimore Boyz. Nadet' wasn't paying them any attention because he received a text from Sister Diane that said good job. He felt good about it because he knew she was speaking for his mom

"Space cadet!"

"Stop calling me that. I can hear you Dee. I just don't care about what you're saying."

"Man, we need a street legal name for you or that's what it's gonna be... Gunz, Wizdom, and Space Cadet! The Baltimore Boyz gonna be the shit."

"Doing what... hustlin? Call me Space Cadet one more time and I'm fuckin' you up. I told you already, I'm not getting in the drug game so I guess I'm not a Baltimore Boy!"

"What the fuck ever man… The Baltimore Boyz are more than hustlin, it's a lifestyle. Loyalty, no snitchin', respect for the code, and everything in between but you already know that shit Day-Day," shouted Dee as he responded.

Everyone on the bus looked at them as they got into each other's face. Nadet' put his hand across Dee's face and pushed it. Ricky jumped between them before he could respond.

"Come on man. Stop this dumb shit! Ya'll like brothers, fuck that…ya'll are brothers."

"Naw, Nadet' thinks he's better than me. That's why you laughed at my ideas and don't want to be a part of The Baltimore Boys, right?!"

Nadet' didn't say anything. He had so much on his mind and his friends didn't seem to understand. Dee's stop was next; he lived a few blocks away from Ricky and Nadet' on Broadway.

"Aight then, this is my stop. I'm gonna check you tomorrow Ricky," said Dee as he looked

Nadet' in the eyes. "You don't have to worry 'bout me anymore."

Dee got off the bus and Ricky looked at Nadet'. He shook his head and smirked because he understood both of them.

"Yo Day-Day, Dee only wants to be a part of something special. That's why he wants you in it so badly. It hurts him when you reject it."

"Man, I ain't got time to babysit Dee. I got problems of my own."

"That's some cold shit," said Ricky.

"Why are you always defending him?"

"I do the same for you because I understand what makes you tick. As far as I can see, he's not mad... he's hurt because you don't want to be down with him. You gotta know who's on your side Day-Day."

"This is our stop," responded Nadet'.

As they got off of the bus they slapped five and went their separate ways. Ricky decided to call Dee to see if he was cool as Nadet' headed home.

Meanwhile... after getting off the bus Dee decided stop pass the corner Caribbean spot. He was still upset about arguing with Nadet'.

"Yo Trevor, gimmie two beef patties!"

"You mean Bitch Patties right?" A voice called out from behind Dee.

"What? Nah, ain't no bitches over here homeboy..." responded Dee as he turned to see who was attempting to call him out. It was Chucky and six other thugged-out niggas.

"That's not what I heard... The Baltimore Bitch Boyz. That's your click right?"

Dee didn't know what to do; they were blocking the only exit and definitely there to handle business. He stood in the corner and put his hand in his jacket like he had a gun.

"Oh you got some heat son-son? Cuz we can loan you one of ours," sarcastically said Chucky as he and every dude with him lifted their jackets to reveal a variety of weaponry.

The people behind the counter ran to the back once they saw all the guns. Dee was silent and terrified. He judged the distance and immediately ran to jump over the counter.

Chucky yelled, "Get that Bitch!"

All his henchmen rushed Dee and caught him at the counter. They swung their fists and weapons at him, beating him across his back and head.

"Drag his ass outside! We gonna take you for a little ride... Gunz." Chucky laughed as he made fun of Dee's Baltimore Boy moniker. They dragged Dee to a black Tahoe, periodically whipping him every time he resisted. Then took everything in his pockets and drove off with him bleeding in the back seat.

Buzz, Buzz, Buzz...

"Is that his phone? Give it to me. Look at this, it's one of your little boy friends," said Chucky. He saw that it was Ricky calling so he answered.

"Hello? Hello?" said Ricky repeatedly to deafening silence.

Chucky motioned for everyone to be quiet. He didn't say anything but breathed heavily into the phone just to fuck with Ricky. Dee yelled out from the back of the truck.

"Ricky! These niggas got me..."

The two dudes sitting on opposite sides of Dee hit him with a gun in the stomach and choked him with a belt. Chucky laughed loudly then spoke into the phone.

"Is this Wisdom? That's what it says on the phone? Wiz, how the fuck you doin'?"

Ricky could hear Dee choking and scuffling in the background.

"Who the fuck is this?"

"It's Chuck nigga. You and the Baltimore Bitches are over before ya'll even begin. This is my territory now… thanks to you. News flash… I ain't Black Rob nigga. I'll erase your ass then go get a line up like nothin' ever happened motherfucker. What!"

Click!

Chucky hung up and threw the cell phone out the window. He was pumped up and ready to prove his point. Chuckey looked at Dee devilishly and instructed the guy driving to get on the highway. "Ya'll ready to have some fun?" he fiendishly asked all his boys.

BLACK BUTTERFLY 2 by FEENIX

CHAPTER **XXII**: "Before Eleven"

Nadet' hurried down the street because once again, he was late getting home and hadn't called. He knew that his grandmother and aunt would be up worried and pissed. It was already ten fifty-five pm but for some reason it just sounded better in his mind if he could say he was in before eleven. When he approached the house, the living room light wasn't on and he was relieved.

"They must have gotten tired and went to bed. Thank God I can deal with them in the morning," he whispered to himself.

Nadet' put his key in the door and slowly opened it being sure not to wake his family. He tripped on some shoes sitting vestibule as he came in. Tip-toe... Tip-toe... Nadet' made his way up to his bedroom undetected. As he took off his shirt and chain he noticed something unusual... total silence and stillness. He started thinking that maybe his grandmother and aunt possibly weren't even home.

"Let me see what the hell is going on," once again talking to himself aloud.

Nadet' quietly walked to his aunt's room and peeked in. There was no one there, so he opened the door all the way to make sure. He then silently walked to his grandmother's room but stopped when he heard a sound downstairs. He paused, looked over the upstairs banister, and listened more carefully.

Creeeee-k! Nadet' heard the basement door shut and immediately got a sick feeling in his stomach. He immediately darted to his grandmother's room, flung the door open and cut on the light. She wasn't there. Nadet' ran downstairs in a panic.

"Grandma! Aunt Jackie! Ya'll down here!"

Nadet' ran to the basement door, flung it open and was hit in the chest with the butt of a gun. He hit the floor with a loud thud and was immediately being dragged down into the basement. Nadet' coughed and clawed as his body hit every step on the way down.

"Get the fuck off me! Somebody help me! Maaaaaaaaaa-a!"

"Shut the fuck up... you little tricky bitch," said a voice in the darkness.

Nadet' could hear his grandmother's and aunt's muffled cries coming out of the basement. When he got to the last step he rolled over and slightly shut his eyes, faking like he was knocked out. Nadet' saw his aunt and grandmother bound and gagged with Drake standing next to them. Drake's henchman, the one that dragged Nadet' down the steps, was in front of him asking what to do next. At that exact moment, Jackie made her chair tip over because she saw Nadet' lying on the ground. Drake looked at her with fury in his eyes and grabbed her by the hair on the floor.

"I should leave you lying on this dirty ass basement floor. Stop all that crying and shit. I want to see the tough bitch that got in my face the last time I was here."

Nadet' suddenly kicked Drake's henchman into him from behind and attempted to run back up the stairs. Drake ordered his henchman go after Nadet'.

"Get him! We gonna put an end to this tonight!"

Nadet' barely made it up the stairs before the henchman grabbed his foot and tripped him at the top. Nadet' kicked his shoe off and continued to claw his way out of the basement door in a panic. When he reached the top of the stairs Drake's henchman was infuriated! He grabbed his gun from the front of his pants and angrily yelled, "Aw, you don't wanna play with uncle Rock no more, lil bitch!"

"No... but I do," calmly said Eboni with Nadet' at her feet.

Bam! Bam!

Shooting him two times in the chest, Rock fell backwards down the steps screaming higher than a woman. Drake turned and saw him flying off the last step into a cabinet in the basement.

"She's her-e," laughed Drake.

Eboni told Nadet' to barricade the front door and windows just in case the police came. She pulled out her other gun and signaled two masked people to move a van out of the alley. Drake began shouting obscenities up the stairs.

"Remember when I use to fuck you on this very floor! I guess it's a dirty ass floor for a dirty ass bitch! What ya think?"

Eboni didn't say anything... she just held both her guns up in the doorway and cocked them so he could hear!

"Oh, that's supposed to scare me? You already gave me a death sentence bitch! I know you pumped me with some toxic shit... didn't you," demanded Drake.

"I figured you would like to take a little bit of John with you as you walk that green mile," responded Eboni.

"So you admit it! I don't believe this shit, you a low down cruddy bitch! That's some fucked..."

"Aw stop cryin' nigga... all bets was off when you raped me fifteen years ago! Did you think I was gonna let you get away with that? I hate you and hope that shit makes you fifty pounds before you die!"

"Alright then, check this out! Now I got five to seven years to make your life hell starting tonight! You didn't count on that, did you bitch?"

Drake grabbed Jackie by the hair again and made her scream in pain. He fired a shot at the steps to make sure Eboni knew not to come down.

"How you want her to get it... in the mouth or ass like you like it? Huh, Eboni? I got the big black steel right here in her face!"

Eboni knew not to show weakness with Drake, it only made him more aggressive. As long as she could keep him talking she was doing well.

"Don't lie to yourself! That gun is by no means your dick nigga! Maybe the trigga is, but that's about it!"

"That's funny. Let's see how funny you are when I pop one or two in your sister or your old ass blind mother! Will it still be funny then? I can see you standing over their graves, responsible for their deaths -just -like -Betty's!"

"Motherfucke-r!" Eboni yelled and let off a hail of shots as she slowly walked down the steps.

Eboni's shots served as cover for the real rescue attempt that came in from the rear basement window. Her people were already in by that time and tackled Drake as he fired back at the steps Eboni was coming down. Once the shots stopped, Eboni came all the way down and saw Drake fighting two of her people. She immediately cut her sister and mother loose then moved them quickly up the steps out of harms way. By that time she was half way up the stairs.

Nadet' yelled down, "People are gathering out front and it looks like the police are comin'!"

"Get Grandma and Jackie out of here! Use the back way!"

Bam! Bam, Bam, Bam! Bam! Bam!

Suddenly Eboni heard a barrage of shots in the darkness of the basement. She turned around and was grabbed by the throat immediately and snatched down the steps. She fought as she fell and made Drake fall with her back down the stairs. He fell on top of her bleeding as his gun slid across the floor.

"I got your ass now! What's the matter... you don't want my blood on you," laughed Drake as he spit blood in her face.

"Get the fuck off of me!!!!" Eboni didn't want him to bleed on her because she knew his blood was contaminated.

Drake got his hands around her throat and began to choke Eboni with all his might so she dug her fingers into his eye sockets. They both tried to roll and squirm out of each other's grip but couldn't.

"Freeze!" a police officer yelled with his gun drawn and flash light in hand.

They didn't even hear him and wouldn't have cared if they did. They hated each other so much that inflicting harm on the other was the only thing they were concerned about.

Running top speed from the back of the basement, Agent JC threw his body into Drake and knocked him off of Eboni. Partially blinded, Drake took a swing at JC and was smashed in the throat with an open hand then slammed to the ground.

"Don't make it hard on yourself," calmly stated JC. "It's over for you."

The cops had their guns on Eboni as she gasped for air on the ground. She could hear Nadet' upstairs fussin' with the cops to let him through. She saw two of her people lying on the floor lifeless and did not want to make the situation any worse by fighting. Eboni rolled over onto her stomach and waited for the cops to take her. One cop put on his rubber gloves and put his knee in her back. He bent her arms roughly and put her in cuffs.

"Fuckin' blood… this is nasty! You better not have any diseases, girly," he remarked as he lifted her by the cuffs to JC's dismay.

"Don't touch her! What the fuck is wrong with you office-r? Aren't you supposed to be under investigation and on administrative duty because of the last incident?"

The officer shrugged his shoulders and smirked like he was untouchable. Eboni looked at the officer's name tag and it said Schwartz, the same cop that Nadet' told her man-handled him. She threw her head backwards into his face and busted his nose while he dropped her back on the ground face first.

JC caught her before she fully hit the ground and said, "Wow... Eboni Machiavelli. Ms. Burton, you are simply amazing. Even I was beginning to doubt that you were still alive."

Without thinking, officer Schwartz yelled, "You black bitch, you broke my nose!"

Everyone gasped when they heard him say that but Eboni just smiled and looked at JC. She said, "I've been called a bitch so much that it doesn't even bother me anymore. Can you make sure my son is alright?"

"No problem, Ms. Burton. I apologize on behalf of law enforcement. People should be presumed innocent until proven guilty and there is no excuse for prejudice. I will personally make sure your family is treated fairly."

JC never got personally involved with any case but this was different. The lady he held in his arms didn't have the demeanor of a killer like all the reports said. Instead, she appeared calm and gentle. JC understood what being provoked could bring out of a person."

THE END.

This book is dedicated to my daughter,

Paris

"You are the sunshine of my day. I love you!"

"A <u>Father</u> is the first relationship that a **daughter** has

with a man. So be an example of the man you want

her to marry!"

BLACK BUTTERFLY 2 by FEENIX

Legal

This book is a work of fiction. Names, characters, places and incidents are products of the author's imagination or are used fictitiously. Any resemblance to actual events or locals or persons, living or dead, is entirely coincidental.

Cover Model: Jennifer Hudson aka "Darelle" as Eboni Burton

Feenix Books LLC
Celebrity Publishing Unlimited
PO Box 66595
Baltimore, Maryland 21239

dantefeenix@gmail.com
http://www.facebook.com/dante.feenix

BLACK BUTTERFLY 2 by FEENIX

SNEAK PREVIEW...

BLACK BUTTERFLY 2 by FEENIX

BLACK BUTTERFLY 3:

"THE Fabulous Baltimore Boyz"

By *FEENIX*

BLACK BUTTERFLY 2 by FEENIX

EBONI'S SONG (the response to Nadet's Song)

One day, I heard **Tupac** say…

"Dear mama, I apologize for all the drama!"

That day he became a **wise man**.

Maybe God took his hand… and squeezed it.

Shit!

Sometimes we don't know where **life** is gonna go

Until we see it!

If you **see pain all the time**, how could you not **be it!**

My name is **Fame.** Don't you dare call this a **game,**

because it's connected… to my **mom,**

I don't want her to know that her baby boy is **long gone.**

A man now, waging war on everyone that did us **wrong**!

Dear Mama, I wanna apologize for all this **drama**…

-Nadet.

BLACK BUTTERFLY 2 by FEENIX

INTRODUCTION:

"SOCIETY SETS UP THE CRIME; THE CRIMINAL JUST COMMITS IT..."

"Dion is in stable condition now. It may take a while before he's one hundred percent but he's gonna be alright for now," said the doctor.

"Yo Dee, man. Can you hear me," asked Rick.

"I can hear you dog but I'm in so much pain right now it's incredible," replied Dee from his hospital bed.

"Yo, did you tell the cops what happened?"

"I'm not telling the cops shit! No snitching... even if it is Chucky that's responsible. I gotta respect the code of the streets even if most niggas don't."

"I know, but we in some real shit now ... huh?"

"Yeah, he said the only reason he didn't kill me is because he wanted to send a message. Some New York dude is supplying him now and they plan to take over."

"Damn, that's real fucked up. So you think he's planning to kill us? Just you and me... or does he know anything about Nadet?"

"Just me and you, I think. He doesn't think Nadet rolls like that... besides he's only seen him once. Did you tell Nadet about this?"

"I left a message on his phone, I don't know..."

"Yeah, I got the motherfuckin message," Nadet slowly opened the bathroom door with watery red eyes. "Now bitch ass Chucky's gonna get the message!" Nadet had been in the bathroom a while listening and thinking.

"Oh my god, Nadet! You scared the shit outta me. How long you been in there?"

"It's **Fame** now, my street legal name is Fame now... because that's all my mother wanted was her piece of the pie. They tryin to take her away from me for no fuckin reason, when all she did was pursue her dreams. They pursue their dreams, but keep us in survival mode all our lives... broke as shit!"

"What are you talking about," asked Rick.

"I'm sorry I rejected you Dee. We're family… they already took my mutha away; I can't let anything happen to you. So check it… let's get rid of Chucky, fund my mother's case, and make the cops pay. I gotta plan son… one hell of a plan. The movement will now be called the militia, this city won't know what hit'em!"

"Yeah, but there's only one problem though… with the addition of **Fame** we can't just be the Baltimore Boyz. It's too small for us. We gonna be **The Fabulous Baltimore Boyz** and fuck all dem niggas up! Let's tell our story from this side of the gun."

Meanwhile… on the other side of town in a dimly lit lawyer's office, Drake and Mr. Greenburg plotted on Eboni's continued demise.

"They want her bad, Drake. She's gotten too much press and this case has exposed the corruption in local law enforcement. She's gotta go down to save the Mayor's neck; the death penalty nothing less," said Mr. Greenburg.

"The Mayor? What does he…"

"Never mind that, they will drop all charges if you turn state witness against her. Just tell them what she did to you with John's blood. If she's smart she'll take a plea."

"I hope I a'int get that AIDS shit from the blood. My test came back negative," said Drake.

"Good, maybe you don't have it but the needle she hit you with did have AIDS ridden blood in it. That my friend; is enough for attempt murder. Damn, what a bitch... you gotta admit it! She must really hate your ass," Mr. Greenburg chuckled to himself.

"Well, she can get in line because this a'int no damn popularity contest. I swear, if I come down with that shit ma-n... What's up with the kid's insurance money?"

"That's over. He can't collect a life insurance policy on a person that's not actually dead, duh! She's up for insurance fraud too, amongst all the other charges."

"I'll testify Greenburg; I hope they bury her ass! It would be a pleasure to see that bitch go down," said Drake.

BLACK BUTTERFLY 3

Now On Amazon & Kindle!

www.ingramcontent.com/pod-product-compliance
Lightning Source LLC
Chambersburg PA
CBHW071152170626
46809CB00002B/864